CONFLICT OF THE HEART

A summer job, as live-in nanny, caring for seven-year-old Ellie seems like a dream for Karen Carmichael. But while Ellie proves a delight, her father, archaeologist Neil Oldson, is hard to get to know. Karen puts his reserve down to pressure from the looming deadline on the nearby Roman site he is managing. But when valuable finds from the site are stolen, her growing feelings for him are thrown into doubt. Then Karen's life is put in danger.

DOROTHY TAYLOR

CONFLICT OF THE HEART

Complete and Unabridged

LINFORD
Leicester

First published in Great Britain in 2008

First Linford Edition
published 2009

British Library CIP Data

Taylor, Dorothy, *1943* –
    Conflict of the heart- -(Linford romance library)
    1. Nannies- -Fiction. 2. Archaeologists- -Fiction.
    3. Archaeological thefts- -Fiction. 4. Romantic
    suspense novels. 5. Large type books.
    I. Title II. Series
    823.9′2–dc22

    ISBN 978–1–84782–835–4

Published by
F. A. Thorpe (Publishing)
Anstey, Leicestershire

Set by Words & Graphics Ltd.
Anstey, Leicestershire
Printed and bound in Great Britain by
T. J. International Ltd., Padstow, Cornwall

This book is printed on acid-free paper

1

Help! The bold heading stood out against the rest of the advertisements in the personal column, catching Karen's eye as soon as she turned the page.

Intrigued, she read on, a smile taking life in her expression as her blue eyes scanned the rest . . . *My dad is going to be very busy for the next three weeks so I need someone to keep me company. Could you do it? My name is Ellie and I'm seven and three-quarters. And I'd like a lady, please.*

Karen chuckled. The child-like plea spoke volumes. Ellie's dad obviously had a great sense of humour to let her word the ad like that and the sense to know it would attract a lot of attention.

The idea of responding to Ellie's appeal flickered into life. She was more than qualified to care for the little girl and it would help take her mind off the last minute cancellation of her holiday.

The huge sense of disappointment she had been trying to shake off for the last two days returned. With a soft sigh she tried not to think about all the plans she and Jenny had made and turned her head to gaze out of the living room window just as a small group of people passed by.

More visitors, she guessed, as the tourists, recognisable by their cameras and guide books, strolled past her small front garden protected by a waist-high sandstone wall. One or two then began pointing out particular houses which had caught their eye.

Several of the party then began to photograph the black and white timber-framed buildings and sandstone cottages forming the centre of the picturesque Cheshire village where she lived all her life.

And if it wasn't for young Johnny Ferguson's lunchbox, she mused wryly, Jenny and I would be doing something similar in France.

She snapped out of her reverie. It was far too gorgeous a day to be stuck inside moping around wondering what might have been. She still had three weeks to fill.

She glanced back at the newspaper and re-read the advertisement. The answer could be right here in her hand? The impulse gripped her. She would give Ellie's father a call. After all she had nothing to lose.

Taking the newspaper through to the hall she placed it alongside the phone on the small table, re-read the contact number and punched it in.

She had just reached the disappointing conclusion no-one was home when her call was finally answered.

'Yes? Who's that?' a loud male voice barked in her ear.

Wincing, Karen jerked her head away from the receiver, frowning at his attitude. This was not the response she had been expecting. It threw her into some confusion. 'Er . . . Karen Carmichael,' she answered feeling a little flustered.

'And what can I do for you?'

Objecting to the continuing abruptness of his manner, she pulled herself together. 'I'm calling about the advertisement in the local paper.'

In the growing silence that followed, she re-checked the number quoted. Perhaps she'd misdialled and the man on the other end was trying to figure out what she was talking about.

She'd give it one more try. If this received the same negative response, she would apologise and put the phone down.

'Help with Ellie . . . ' she offered.

The silence was immediately broken. 'Oh, I see,' he exclaimed. 'I'm with you now.'

Karen raised her eyebrows. If this was Ellie's father, the little girl wasn't exaggerating. He appeared busy to the point of abstraction.

'Sorry . . . but the — '

'Post has already been filled?' She jumped in, second guessing and feeling a sense of relief. It was just as well.

4

She'd changed her mind about the personality of the man behind the ad and wished she hadn't even bothered to make the call in the first place.

'No, no. Not at all,' the voice came back swiftly. 'The advertising department told me it wouldn't appear until next Wednesday. Obviously they managed it sooner. Hence the confusion on my part.'

'Oh, I see,' she responded unenthusiastically.

'As a matter of fact,' he continued, 'you're the first person to ring.'

A warmer manner now replaced his initial air of preoccupation and Karen found herself responding to it. Maybe this could work out after all.

'So you're interested in helping Ellie and I out . . . Miss . . . er Mrs?'

'Karen Carmichael," she repeated with a grimace of impatience that he had already forgotten her name. 'I'm twenty-six, unmarried, with no ties,' she added. There now he was completely in the picture.

'Er, yes . . . right. Names Neil Oldson,' the voice suddenly supplied in return.

Neil Oldson? Her brow puckered a little. His name had a familiar ring, but from where she couldn't recall.

'Do you have any child care experience, Miss Carmichael?'

'I work at the village nursery. It's in the book under that name. If you'd care to ring Mrs Johnson, the owner, I'm sure she would be happy to give you a character reference and confirm my experience.'

'Right.'

She sensed he was writing this down.

'But if you're employed there?'

'I'm on two weeks' leave,' she explained, sensing his confusion. 'The following week the nursery will be closed for some refurbishment. So I have three free weeks ahead of me.'

'I see,' she heard him murmur. And then, 'But surely you're in need of a break from children?'

The surprise in his voice had her smiling. 'There's been a problem with my holiday. It was a last minute cancellation,' she expanded. 'My friend, who works at the nursery too, had an accident.'

'Not serious, I hope.

'She tripped over a lunchbox that had somehow found its way on to the floor and suffered a badly sprained ankle. Serious enough to put a stop to the backpacking tour of France we'd planned. It's not the type of holiday I'd like to do alone.'

'Hmm. I imagine not. So you're at a loose end?'

His comment made her enquiry sound superficial. She had to put him right.'

'Not at all,' she exclaimed defensively. 'I do have other alternatives.'

Well maybe not right at this minute, she accepted, but she would think of something before the day was over. And if this call continued to go the way it had begun, she would definitely have to make some other choices.

'The appeal of the wording of your

advertisement gave me the idea to ring,' she added. 'There seemed an air of desperation about it.'

'You could say that.' The tone of his voice indicated he'd got the message. 'Ellie and I hoped it would stand out. So thanks for responding.'

'You're welcome.' With this show of appreciation Karen's mood lightened. Then her smile returned as she recalled Ellie's literal description. 'Believe me, Mr Oldson, caring for one seven and three-quarters little girl will be a break from working with a large group of toddlers to pre-school four-year-olds. Not that I'm complaining,' she added hastily. 'I love my work. I have a niece and nephew close to your daughter's age and several of my friends have older children, so I'm well used to them, too.'

'Hmm . . . sounds fine,' he responded thoughtfully. 'Is there any possibility you could call round today for a chat? We're just a mile or so outside the village. You can meet Ellie.'

'Yes, I can do that.' She checked her

watch. It wouldn't take long to change out of her jeans and T-shirt into something a little more formal and secure her wayward hair up with a grip. 'Would two o'clock suit you?'

'Perfect. Ellie's having lunch with her grandparents but should be back any time now. I'll see you later then.'

'Mr Oldson?' Karen questioned swiftly, sensing he was about to ring off. 'Where exactly do I find you . . . and Ellie?'

Could this man be more distracted, she wondered.

'What?' His exclamation was followed by something sounding suspiciously like the slapping of a forehead.

She quickly covered her mouth with her hand to suppress a giggle. Neil Oldson's distracted manner was becoming more entertaining than off-putting.

'Of course,' he said. 'The address would be of help, wouldn't it? Right. The house is called Mile End.'

Karen reached for a pen as he proceeded to give her directions.

'It's a biggish sandstone structure set

a fair way off Backhall Lane,' he added. 'But you can't miss it. If you're coming in off the top road, you'll see a farm first. Hartley's the owner. Take the first right after that.'

'I know Hartley's farm,' she confirmed. 'Sounds like you're not far from where all the excitement took place recently.'

When pieces of Roman pottery had been uncovered by the utilities company laying a new pipeline, the local press had really gone to town. There had also been a feature on the regional TV news. It had caused quite a stir in the village and speculation of what else might be unearthed had been rife.

'Couldn't be closer,' he said. 'Mile End backs directly on to it. Actually, I was asked to give my opinion about the finds. I'm an archaeologist. The university I'm attached to has taken an interest. Since then I've been in charge of the dig.'

'Oh, I see.' That was it. She must have heard his name in all the media coverage.

The picture was becoming clearer.

Her initial bemusement at his pre-occupied manner turned to understanding. Despite the attractive timbre of his voice, he was coming across as the proverbial absent-minded professor.

2

A little later after showering and changing into a lightweight navy blue suit and short-sleeved cream shirt, Karen left her small end-terraced cottage and walked around to the side where she parked her car.

As she drove out of the village, she wondered again about the man she would soon be meeting. From what the advertisement implied, Neil Oldson was a single parent. Widowed . . . divorced?

She decided it was none of her business and concentrated instead on where the route would eventually take her.

She'd known most of the area all her life but after passing Hartley's farm with its black and white grazing dairy herds and huge milking sheds, the landscape became unfamiliar along the lane she had been instructed to take.

Around the next bend the lane took a sudden dip and the countryside opened up before her. Up ahead and over to her left, the grey slated roofs and darkly pink sandstone structure of an old country house was partly visible through a random screen of pine trees.

Alongside it she noticed an empty paddock. Several oblong trenches scarred the expanse of grass, showing evidence there had been quite a lot of digging done recently.

A little anxious now as to how the interview would go, she steered her car on to the gravel driveway, passing the tall cast-iron gates standing open in welcome.

Colourful, carefully-tended borders were set either side of the drive which eventually swept into a wide curve when it opened up in front of the house.

A Land Rover was parked to one side of the sandstone porch separating the double-fronted square bay windows. A small red car and a silver people carrier stood on the other side.

Karen chose a space alongside the Land Rover and switched off her engine. With a sense of increasing anticipation she climbed out of her car.

After securing the car door, she was aware of movement in the corner of her eye. She glanced up and was surprised by the sudden appearance of a small child dressed in pink cropped trousers and matching T-shirt running out of the porch and over in her direction.

Her dark plaited hair, secured with pink bobbles, bounced against her shoulders as she drew up to a halt in front of Karen. Her large grey eyes were shining with excitement.

'Hello, I'm Ellie,' she announced a little breathlessly. 'Are you Miss Carmichael? Dad told me you were coming so I've been watching from the window waiting for your car.'

'That's sweet of you.' Karen returned Ellie's smile, touched by her admission and liking at once the small oval face with its scattering of freckles bridging her nose. 'Yes, I am. My other name is Karen. You can call me that if you like.'

Ellie nodded. 'Yes, please. Dad's talking on the phone but I made him understand you were here, so he won't be a minute.'

'That's all right, Ellie.' Another applicant for the post, she wondered. 'I expect your dad is a very busy man.'

Ellie rolled her eyes dramatically and folded her arms against her chest. 'Well he's a professor,' she said with more than a hint of pride, 'and just about the busiest person in the whole world.'

Karen hid a smile. 'Really!'

'Ellie Oldson,' came the gentle rebuke from behind, 'that has to be an exaggeration.'

'Dad!' While Ellie spun round and turned her attention to her father, Karen glanced up with some interest.

When she saw the owner of the voice a short distance away, her heart suddenly picked up a pace.

At over six feet tall, Neil Oldson had the lean, muscular build of a man in his mid to late thirties who was used to physical work.

He was dressed casually in jeans and a pale blue shirt open at the neck. His sleeves were rolled up over deeply tanned forearms, showing he spent a lot of time outdoors.

When he reached the side of her car, it was then she saw where Ellie had inherited her colouring. His eyes were the same silver grey and fringed with the thickest of lashes. His dark hair was a little over-long, and had a slight curl to it, but it did not detract from his overall masculinity.

'Miss Carmichael.' When he offered his hand, Karen sensed there was something forced about his smile. His mind seemed somewhere else. 'Thank you for coming,' he added rather formally.

'Pleased to meet you, Professor Oldson.' Her initial reaction to his rugged looks changed to one of wariness as her hand was given a firm shake.

'I take it Ellie has already introduced herself.' He glanced down at his daughter.

Then Karen caught the look of affection that passed between them as Ellie slipped beneath his arm and he placed it around her shoulders in a protective way.

So there was another side to him. He wasn't a total cold fish, after all.

'Yes, she has,' she confirmed, smiling at the child.

'In that case,' Neil said, 'let's not waste any more time. Come on through to the kitchen,' he invited, gesturing with his other hand. 'We can chat in there while I make some coffee.'

'Thank you. That would be nice.'

'We have only recently moved into Mile End,' he said as he fell into step alongside her. Ellie slipped between them and took his hand. 'It belonged to my late godmother. We have a live-in housekeeper, Martha Peters, and her husband, John, who sees to the gardens and anything else that needs doing.

They had been with Constance for years and thankfully agreed to stay on.'

'It's Mr and Mrs Peters' day off today,' Ellie joined in, looking up at Karen. 'Dad says Mrs Peters has too much to do besides look after me. Even though she lets me help her make butterfly cakes and buns and Mr Peters shows me which weeds to pull out when I help him in the garden or the vegetable patch.'

Above Ellie's head Neil threw Karen something resembling a smile.

She responded with her natural friendliness. Things were looking up, she decided.

'Mr and Mrs Peters are close to retirement age,' he explained in an undertone. 'Although their daughter, Valerie, is coming in to help over the next three weeks,' he shrugged, 'I couldn't impose.'

Karen got his meaning. 'I understand,' she said softly.

'You'll meet them — ' He broke off. Sensing what he was about to say,

Karen's hopes of securing the position rose.

'Providing of course . . . ' To her surprise he looked a little uncomfortable. 'Anyway, like I said, it's a great help having them on hand.' He gestured into the porch towards the open front door. 'After you . . . '

She did as instructed and as soon as she stepped over the threshold and into the roomy, square hall, she immediately felt at home.

'Passageway on the right,' Neil prompted when she paused uncertain of which way to go. 'The kitchen's at the end.'

'I'll show you,' Ellie offered and skipped off ahead. 'It's down here.'

'Help yourself to a chair.' Neil pointed over to two squidgy armchairs placed either side of the old fashioned range, after they followed Ellie into the traditional sunlit kitchen.

While she skirted the long refectory table dominating the centre space, Neil walked over to one of the counters to see to the coffee.

Once seated, she began to relax. Despite the coolness of his manner he seemed to be going out of his way to make her feel at home. Which was nice, she decided as she watched him pick up the kettle and fill it with water.

Ellie went over to the fridge and took out a small carton of fresh orange juice then slid on to one of the chairs at the table.

As she concentrated on piercing the carton with the small straw that came with it, Neil leaned back against the counter and folded his arms in front of him.

Karen smiled to herself. Like father, like daughter, she reflected, recalling Ellie doing the same outside.

Neil glanced over to where she was sitting. 'D'you come from around these parts, Miss Carmichael?' he asked.

'Yes, I do,' she confirmed. 'My family has lived here for generations, although my parents have recently retired to Spain. Dad suffers from arthritis and the climate is kinder there. My elder brother, David, lives in the next village.'

'You mentioned his children when we talked before.'

Karen was impressed. So he wasn't as abstracted as she'd concluded.

'And you work at the local nursery?'

'I do. The Village Nursery,' she repeated just in case he'd forgotten the name.

'I'd like to go to school here,' Ellie piped up. She gave her father a pleading look. 'Couldn't I do that, Dad, after the summer holidays?'

Ellie was given a wry smile in response. He should smile more often, Karen reflected. It suits him.

'If we do decide to come to live here permanently, of course you will,' Neil promised his daughter. 'But at the moment you know I've other things on my mind.'

'And that's why you're going to be so busy, and need someone to look after me,' Ellie finished for him.

'That's right,' he nodded. 'But once

the report's written, we'll spend time doing whatever you want to do. So while Miss Carmichael and I have a little chat,' he skilfully got down to business, 'I think you should take your juice up to your room and start writing a list of what those things might be.'

'Great idea, Dad.' Ellie threw Karen a grin before wriggling off the chair. 'See you later, Karen.'

Enjoying the child's sunny disposition, and ignoring Neil's raised brows at his daughter's familiarity, Karen responded in kind. 'See you later, Ellie.'

'I hope you don't mind,' she said turning to him once they were alone. 'It was my idea. Miss Carmichael sounded far too formal in a home situation.'

'I expect you're right.' A brief smile lit his face again and suddenly she saw him in a different light. Then it was lost almost immediately to a frown. 'But I don't want her taking liberties.'

'I don't think she's the type.'

'Actually,' Neil said, 'you're right. She isn't.' He poured the coffee into two blue-banded mugs and brought them over on a tray.

Neil took the other armchair. After he'd taken a few pulls from his mug, he looked across at her.

She immediately found herself growing ridiculously self-conscious under her prospective employer's penetrating grey gaze.

'You must be very disappointed about your cancelled holiday,' he said after a moment's silence.

She shrugged slightly. 'Well, yes I was but these things happen and I'm over it now. Whereas poor Jenny can only sit and nurse her ankle for the next few weeks and brood. I've been making regular visits to keep her spirits up, but she's feeling very frustrated at the moment.'

'I can imagine. Well I'm sure she appreciates you calling round. Right. I'll get straight to the point.'

His sudden change to a business-like tone had her straightening subconsciously in her chair.

'The next few weeks are crucial,' he began. 'I'm convinced there is an archaeological site here that will turn out to be of significant importance.'

'You know that from just some pieces of pottery?' Karen exclaimed, impressed by his expertise.

He hesitated and for a moment she sensed he was considering his answer.

'Since the utilities company left, there have been a few other promising finds indicating we could have a Roman villa here. It would be the first discovered in the area,' he said rather guardedly. 'So you can appreciate the possible importance. Two of my colleagues, who have been working the site with me, are of the same mind.

'But time is limited and more people are needed if we're going to make real headway. Hartley's agreeable to the dig continuing on his land and luckily what we uncovered recently appears to be running back into the paddock as well as extending further out into his field. What I need now is funding approval from the university authorities to carry on. Hence,' he grimaced, 'the urgency to put my case in writing.'

'I see.' Karen's expression softened. 'And that's the reason you need help with Ellie.'

He nodded. 'That's right.'

She sensed the same change in his manner she had witnessed outside when he had placed his arm around Ellie. It was becoming clear to her how much he cared for his daughter.

Then his business-like manner returned and she put aside her thoughts. 'Caroline and Simon, my two colleagues, are staying here for the next three weeks. The least I could do was offer them a roof over their heads for giving up their own time. Thankfully, with Valerie's help, Martha is quite happy to accommodate three extra guests.'

Three? Karen pondered. It suddenly struck her. Would the third person be Ellie's companion?

'Because there is such easy access to the site,' he continued, grabbing her attention again before she could query this, 'it's vital word of these finds does not reach the media and the wrong kind of person is attracted to it.'

After regarding her steadily for a moment longer, he added, 'You're not the wrong kind of person to be entrusted with this information, are you, Miss Carmichael?'

3

Karen felt her colour rise with angry indignance that Neil Oldson could consider her untrustworthy. With cold regard she met the steely grey gaze now challenging her.

It took some effort but she bit back on the offence he'd caused, knowing it would do no good to lose her temper.

'Surely by telling me about the discoveries,' she responded stiffly, 'you have answered your own question, Professor Oldson?'

There was a bitter taste in her mouth and a huge sense of disappointment that now after meeting such a sweetie as Ellie, she wouldn't be seeing her again. For there was no way on earth she could work for her insensitive father.

In an atmosphere laden with uncomfortable silence, Karen reached for her bag. It was time to go.

'Miss Carmichael . . . Karen?'

She glanced up at him. Was that a hint of self-reproach she was hearing?

He'd moved further forward almost to the edge of his chair. His grey eyes wary, his expression grim. 'I've offended you.'

'You could say that.' She stared back icily at him.

He had the good grace to look concerned as he placed his coffee mug by his feet.

'Believe me it wasn't intentional,' he said, looking back at her with some concern. Then he frowned. 'I have so much on my mind at the moment. But still,' he dismissed his defense with a gesture of his hand, 'that's no excuse and I'm sorry. I could have chosen my words more carefully.'

The apologetic smile lifting one corner of his mouth almost worked . . . but not quite.

'I agree. You could.' Her blue eyes flashed with continuing icy regard as she refused to be swayed. 'I'm not used to having my honesty questioned. I assume you've not been in touch with Mrs Johnson.'

He looked uncomfortable. 'Got tied up with other things.'

She couldn't believe he could be so remiss. This man needed looking after as much as his daughter.

She thrust her mug towards him, signalling their meeting was over and got up from the chair.

'Please. You're not leaving?' There was an edge of panic to his voice. He scrambled to his feet and took the mug off her, quickly placing it on the tray along with his own.

'Yes, I think it best that I do,' she informed him firmly. 'I don't see the point of continuing this interview. Thank you for the coffee and — '

'But Ellie seems to have taken such a shine to you,' he interrupted.

As I have to her, Karen admitted silently. But there was nothing more to say.

She shrugged. 'I'm sure you'll find

someone Ellie will like just as much. But you must check people's references, Professor Oldson. I can't stress enough how important it is that you do.'

'Neil, please. Let's cut the formalities.' Blocking her way, he raked his fingers through his hair. 'OK, I was tactless. I can see that now. Working an eighteen hour day seems to be affecting my social skills and I apologise. Can we begin this conversation again?'

Was it his look of remorse, or his delightful daughter that made her change her mind? Right then she wasn't sure but with some wariness she found herself reconsidering his request.

'Give me an idea of Ellie's routine; her likes and dislikes,' she suggested, 'and I'll see what I can do.'

'Thank you.'

The sincerity in his voice clinched it. She sat down again.

A relieved looking Neil followed suit.

He then went on to give her some idea of how Ellie liked to spend her time.

When he mentioned the amount he was prepared to pay her for looking after his daughter, she tried not to raise her brows at the size.

'A little family history might also be of help to you,' he suggested. 'My wife, Sarah, died in childbirth.' Karen noticed a flicker of sorrow darken his eyes. 'There were unexpected complications. Naturally, Ellie has never known her mother and I'm always conscious of having to make up for her loss. But sometimes juggling my work,' he gave her a rueful look, 'and trying to be a full-time parent . . . ' he tailed off.

'Can be difficult,' she finished for him, with understanding.

As he rose a little more in her estimation, Karen gave him a sympathetic look. It was clear he'd done a wonderful job to be able to cope with his own loss while raising Ellie to be the lively, outgoing child she was.

'She's a credit to you,' she said, sincerely.

'Thanks.' His expression lightened. 'But it's not all down to me. My mother and stepfather have been an enormous help. But recently she was diagnosed with a heart condition . . . nothing serious,' he expanded in response to Karen's expression of sympathy, 'but you must know how draining children can be sometimes.'

'Don't I just,' she smiled, thinking of the times she had arrived home wrung out after a particularly exhausting day at the nursery. 'But I'm sure caring for Ellie for three weeks will be enjoyable. And the hours?'

He frowned. 'Didn't I stipulate that in the advertisement? The post has to be live-in.'

So she'd been right about the third guest, she reflected. 'No,' she said. 'No mention was made of it being live-in.' She remembered the details clearly.

He shook his head at his own shortcomings then a troubled look returned to his face as he frowned across at her. 'It's not a problem for you is it, staying here for three weeks?'

She thought it over for a minute. It

hadn't entered her head she would be required to stay at the house.

'No,' she considered slowly.

'I need to be on site by six every morning if I'm going to make any headway. Ellie is an early riser, but not that early. She usually wakes around seven. Martha will give her breakfast, of course, but I need someone to make sure she's,' he raised a brow, 'you know . . . presentable.'

Karen smiled. 'I understand.'

'Then in the evenings after dinner, I have to get down to writing my report. So you see I need someone on hand just in case anything unexpected comes up.'

'Only too clearly,' she cut in appreciatively, wondering how long he could keep up a work-load like that.

He bent forward again in his chair. Fingers linked, he rested his forearms on his knees and gazed across at her; the light of commitment steeling his eyes.

'This project matters a lot to me,' he

said. 'These days, it all boils down to funding whether or not a dig will be extended. At the moment it doesn't look hopeful. That's why the report is vital. If we could just find something of high quality status to back up my gut feeling,' he shrugged.

'I see,' she said.

'Knowing Ellie's needs are being catered for will enable me to give it my best.' His half smile was back and she warmed to it but behind the now softer grey eyes looking back at her, she could see his desperate need to achieve his aims.

She was won over completely. 'I'll take good care of her, Neil,' she confirmed.

The look he gave her said it all. 'Appreciate it,' he said gruffly. 'I'll make it up to her, believe me.'

'Oh, I do,' she grinned, wanting to lighten the atmosphere.

Now he had her acceptance, Neil's manner became more relaxed but there was still an air of formality about him she wished he could lose.

'Would you like to see the rest of the house . . . the gardens? Get a feel of the place?'

'Yes, please.'

'I'll just give Ellie a call. Come along with me.' He got to his feet and Karen did the same, keen to take up his suggestion.

But just then Ellie came bouncing back into the kitchen, list in hand. 'Finished, Dad,' she announced loudly, thrusting a piece of paper at him with an eager grin.

'Perfect timing,' he exclaimed, 'we were just coming to look for you.' He took the paper from under his nose and gave it a quick glance before tucking it into his shirt pocket. 'That's fine, sweetheart,' he smiled down at her. 'I'll keep it safe, don't worry.'

He placed an arm around her shoulder. 'Now, what d'you think? I've some good news for you. Can you guess what it is?'

Ellie gazed up at him and shook her head.

Neil shot Karen a look before turning back to his daughter. 'Karen has agreed to come and keep us company.'

Ellie's eyes lit up. 'Has she?' She turned to Karen. 'I'm glad,' she said a little shyly.

'Thank you, Ellie,' Karen chuckled.

'So shall we show her around?'

'Too right, Dad.' Ellie enthused. She turned back to Karen. 'Mrs Peters showed me the room you'll be using. Would you like to see it?'

Karen's smile broadened. Ellie's enthusiasm was infectious. 'Yes please.'

'You'll be next door to Caroline,' Neil said once they reached the second floor landing. 'It's this one, here.' He paused for a moment on the threshold of the third room down from the broad staircase. Several more ran off in the opposite direction. 'I hope you'll find it comfortable.'

Karen followed Ellie inside and glanced with some curiosity around the sunlit surroundings.

The room was a good size and very

welcoming. Pretty pale green curtains stirred gently in the cool summer breeze drifting in through the open leaded windows. Against the backdrop of creamy floral wallpaper and dusky pink carpet, highly polished mahogany furniture gleamed. And the bed, she decided, looked very comfortable.

She could tell Ellie was waiting for her opinion. 'It's a very pretty room, Ellie. I'm sure I'm going to like it here.'

Ellie beamed. 'You can come and see mine now, if you like.'

'Hope it's tidy, young lady,' Neil teased.

Ellie glanced up at her father. 'Oops,' she said putting a hand to her mouth.

Neil made a show of checking his watch. 'You've got two minutes.'

'Yes, Dad.' With that she shot out of the open doorway and disappeared.

'Would you like to come over to the window, while we're waiting,' Neil suggested. 'There's a clear view of the dig from up here.'

Immediately the view took her breath

away. Beyond the sweeping lawns and wide borders of the rear garden, the quilted fields of the Cheshire plain, dotted here and there with the darker green of copse or woodland, seemed to roll on for ever. And in the far distance the hazy blue backdrop of the distant Welsh hills formed an impressive skyline.

'There's Simon and Caroline.' Neil pointed down over to the right. 'Can you see them? They're just beyond the farmer's hedge.'

Karen followed his direction. A combination of gnarled elder trees and hawthorn hedging separated Mile End's grounds and the farmland but it was easy to see Neil's colleagues who she judged to be around her own age. They were kneeling in one of several dark trenches marking the fallow field, both scraping back the earth.

Caroline's blonde hair was tied back in one long plait to prevent it sweeping over her face as she worked.

Simon's colouring appeared similar to Neil's.

'They've been good friends of mine for several years now,' he said. 'The support they're giving me at the moment is invaluable.' He glanced back at her. 'Would you like to visit the site . . . see how the work's progressing?'

'Yes, I'd like that.' Was this his way of reinforcing his trust in her, she wondered. 'But I think I should see Ellie's room first,' she reminded him lightly.

A little later, beneath the hot sun, Neil guided her through an access gap in the hedge. Ellie had raced ahead of them and was wandering around the field stooping down here and there to pick wild flowers.

'Caroline . . . Simon,' Neil called. 'I've someone here I'd like you to mect.'

As the couple turned their heads in response, Neil said, 'Come on over, Karen. You can take a look at what we've been doing.'

By the time they reached the trench, Caroline and Simon had stepped out of it, both arching their backs to ease their tired muscles.

They looked at Karen with some curiosity but their overall manner appeared friendly.

'This is Karen,' Neil explained. 'She will be looking after Ellie for the next three weeks.'

Understanding lit both faces. 'Hi, Karen,' Caroline offered her hand first. When she noticed the streaks of dirt on her palm, she took it back and rubbed it against her canvas shorts. 'Sorry,' her white teeth flashed against her tanned complexion. 'One of the minuses of the job, I'm afraid.'

'Pleased to meet you.' Karen greeted Caroline warmly.

'And knees,' Simon joined in with a grin. 'Hi there,' he nodded, raising his palms to show his were just as grubby.

'Hi, Simon,' Karen echoed.

'You should see us when it's wet,' he joked. 'By the end of the day we look like we've been in a rugby scrum.'

Apt, Karen mused as she chuckled at Simon's description. His stocky build hinted he enjoyed field sports.

She was instantly won over by the couple.

'So this is where the pottery was found.' She couldn't resist a peek inside the trench.

'That's right,' Neil nodded. 'And yesterday we uncovered something far more significant.' He pointed down to where Caroline and Simon had been working. 'The remains of several walls.'

'Really.' Expecting a neat row of stone blocks or bricks, Karen's brow puckered at the partly-exposed irregular runs of rubble Neil was pointing to.

She frowned up at him. 'Those are walls?' she doubted.

'Certainly are. Well, actually they're the inner cores,' he explained. 'The outer stones or bricks tended to be recycled after the Romans left.'

'Oh, I see,' she nodded, becoming more interested as he explained.

'And look what else we've just uncovered,' Caroline said eagerly. She bent down and picked up a small wooden tray and offered it to Neil.

He picked out what looked to Karen like a piece of terracotta pot and showed it to her.

'More broken roof tiles,' he confirmed with satisfaction. 'Ah,' he exclaimed, 'what have we here.' He began to examine several small square pieces of stone. Then he shot Caroline and Simon a very pleased look. 'Tesserae,' he exclaimed. 'I just knew we'd come across some soon.'

Caroline and Simon exchanged amused looks at Neil's reaction. 'It's getting better all the time,' Simon said.

Then Neil noticed Karen was again looking puzzled. 'Mosaics,' he explained. 'Used sometimes to great effect as floor tiles. So it's looking very much like we have a building here.'

'Your villa?' she suggested, caught up in the general excitement.

Neil considered what she'd said. 'We'll have to do a bit more exploring yet. But I'm very much hopeful that's what we've got.'

'I'll keep my fingers crossed for you,' she said and meant it.

'Thanks,' he acknowledged. 'We need all the help we can get.' His eyes then held hers until she looked away feeling strangely shaken.

To overcome this reaction to him, she glanced at her watch. It came as a shock to see she'd been there for over two hours. 'If that's everything,' she braced herself to meet those disturbing grey eyes once more, 'I suppose I should get back home and make a start on some packing.'

'Of course,' Neil said. 'We've monopolised enough of your time.'

'And you're really coming to stay tomorrow?' After her initial excitement, Ellie's voice now held a hint of disbelief as she and Neil walked Karen back to her car.

'That's right, Ellie,' she told her, touched by the child's hopeful grey eyes. 'I'll be here until your dad finishes his report.'

'Great!' Ellie shouted. 'We'll be able to do all kinds of exciting things every day. Can I have my list back, Dad?'

'Whoa. Hold on.' Neil protested good-humouredly. 'If Karen feels she's going to be run ragged, she might just change her mind.'

'You won't, will you?' Ellie shot Karen an anxious look.

'Of course, I won't,' Karen quickly reassured her. Then she gave Neil a chiding glance. His grimace of remorse held her eyes again, long enough for her to feel her cheeks grow warm.

Slightly flustered she turned her attention back to his daughter. 'I'll be here at eight o'clock tomorrow morning. That's a promise.'

'I'll wait at the window and these are for you.' Ellie thrust the pink clover, golden buttercups and white daisies towards her.

Karen was touched. 'Why thank you, Ellie. They're lovely.'

'And thank you, Karen,' she heard Neil say. She glanced up to see he was

44

offering his hand.

With a feeling of satisfaction she responded to the unspoken gesture that their contract was sealed. 'Bye then,' she said, 'I'll see you tomorrow.'

There was no way, she considered, the next three weeks would be as exciting as the backpacking holiday she'd been looking forward to with Jenny. But the thought of spending time with Ellie instead brought a smile to her face.

Then it faded into thoughtfulness when she considered the child's father.

Immediately the mental image of his disturbing grey eyes returned and unexpectedly, her stomach turned over. Extremely attractive he may be but she was still to get the measure of the man.

4

Neil stepped out of the trench as Karen approached with Ellie. 'Karen. It's good to see you.' His words were pleasant enough and his smile disturbed her butterflies again, but she sensed it was still an effort for him to be this friendly.

'Hi, Karen.' In contrast, Caroline and Simon had no trouble at all and greeted her warmly.

'I hope we're not interrupting,' she began after returning their greeting. 'But Martha said you wanted to see me as soon as I'd unpacked.'

'That's right,' Neil confirmed, his presence within the small group as dominating as it had been the day before. 'Just wanted to be sure you're settled in.'

The breeze picked up. It ruffled his dark hair away from his face and sent his black T-shirt rippling against his chest and once more she was aware of the breadth of his shoulders, his muscular build . . . and his nearness.

She quickly shook her mind free, thankful he had no idea of what she was thinking.

'She made you welcome?'

'Very much so,' she confirmed. 'I also met her husband, John, and daughter, Valerie. John helped with my cases. And then Ellie,' she smiled down at her, 'worked hard helping me unpack.'

Ellie was hopping from one foot to another and Karen could tell she was impatient to be off.

'And now Karen's going to look at my list of what to do and we're going to choose something,' Ellie announced. 'Don't worry, Dad,' she grinned at Neil's sudden look of concern. 'I made another list before I went to bed in case you lost yours.'

'Off you go then,' he said above the general laughter Ellie's comment had caused. 'Have a good time and we'll see you when you get back.'

Later that afternoon while Ellie sat at the kitchen table drawing a picture of the pleasure boat trip they had taken earlier on the river Dee in Chester, Karen and Martha had made themselves comfortable in the two armchairs and were enjoying a cup of tea.

'The day couldn't have been more perfect,' she enthused. 'We had a wonderful time on the river, didn't we Ellie?'

Ellie nodded. 'Can we go again tomorrow?'

'What? So soon.' Karen said.

'I think you should leave it for at least another week,' Martha joined in. 'I'm sure Karen has already thought of something for tomorrow.'

'Lots of things,' Karen agreed. 'But we'll look at your list again later and decide.'

She had enjoyed every minute of the time spent with Ellie today, pleased she had remembered to take her camera. An idea was building in her mind. Over the next three weeks she would keep a record of their time together and fill an album with the photographs. It would make, she hoped, a memorable gift for Ellie.

Martha then returned to the subject of her three grandchildren, the next, her son and daughter-in-law's was due in about three weeks' time. Her proud chatter about them all was suddenly interrupted by the sound of the doorbell.

'I'll get it.' Ellie immediately put down her felt-tipped pen and wriggled around off her chair.

'Just hold on a minute, young lady,' Martha grumbled good-naturedly. While she heaved herself up from the arm-chair, Ellie stopped in her tracks. 'Let me see who it is first.'

A distant squeal coming from the direction of the hall had Karen turning her head. She frowned. That sounded like Ellie. Aware of her responsibilities, she grabbed a hand towel and quickly dried her hands.

She was halfway across the kitchen

when the door was flung open and there was Ellie, perched high upon a man's shoulders, her hands clasped around his head.

'Mind your head,' he instructed as he manoeuvred them both through the doorway.

While Karen watched with a little consternation, Ellie ducked down, giggling as he carried her into the kitchen.

'Right. Down you come,' he said.

Karen watched with some relief as he then lifted Ellie up and swept her back down to her feet. Giggling, she held on to his hands until she had regained her balance.

'There's too much excitement going on here for someone close to her bedtime,' Martha warned, her brown eyes full of merriment. 'Cup of tea, Tony?'

'A coffee would be even nicer,' he said. 'But I'll take a rain check for now. See Neil first.'

His voice, Karen noticed, had a slight mid-Atlantic accent.

He looked across and smiled at Karen. It was an infectious smile and she found herself responding. At the same time wondering who this tall, blond stranger, dressed casually in a cream polo shirt and khaki chinos was.

'Ellie's just been insisting I come and meet you,' he said. 'So you're Karen, her temporary nanny.'

'Karen's not my nanny, Uncle Tony,' Ellie protested, before he could introduce himself. She rolled her eyes. 'I'm not a baby. Karen's my friend.'

He gave his niece a mock sheepish look. 'Of course you're not. You must be what . . . five by now.'

Ellie squealed again, enjoying his teasing. 'I'm not. I'm seven and three-quarters. You know that.'

Karen chuckled as she watched their interaction. Whoever Uncle Tony was, he was certainly fun and he obviously had a fan in Ellie.

'Of course you are,' he grinned, 'just checking.' He walked over to Karen. 'Tony Brookes,' he offered his hand.

'Neil's stepbrother.'

Could two men be any different, she wondered.

'Hello, Tony, Karen Carmichael,' she greeted, smiling back at him. 'Nice to meet you. I didn't realise Neil had a brother.'

'Oh he tries to keep it quiet. Or me quiet,' his smile broadened and his eyes flashed. 'You could say we're not on the same wavelength. So where is he. Busy working I expect.'

'He's down on the site.' Karen explained. She glanced at the clock. 'I believe he breaks off at six, so he shouldn't be long now.'

'Just time enough for me to stroll down and see how things are progressing then,' Tony said. 'Dad and Heather were telling me about Neil's discoveries. I'm staying with them for a few weeks,' he added. 'They're very up about his work. Couldn't have worked out better, could it. Inheriting the house one minute, ancient stuff being found the next.'

Sensing for a brief moment there seemed to be a slight edge to Tony's amiable manner, Karen didn't know what to say.

'I'll show you, Uncle Tony,' Ellie grabbed his hand.

'What about my little helper,' Martha called over.

Ellie's shoulders slumped. She pulled a face. 'I promised I'd set the dining table,' she explained to her uncle.

'Well you can't back down on a promise, Ellie,' Tony told her. He hunkered down to her level. 'How about I take you and Karen out one day while I'm here, to make up for it.'

While Karen raised her brows, Ellie's eyes shone. 'Would you, Uncle Tony? Remember you promised next time you came to stay with Grandma and Grandad I could see your plane and you'd take me flying.'

'So I did. Now that would make for a good day out, wouldn't it? But I'll have to check with your dad first.' He straightened up again. 'And Karen, too.'

He flashed her a long look.

'Let's see what Neil says,' she said diplomatically.

'Of course.' With that he went over to Martha who was beginning to prepare the vegetables. He placed his hands on her shoulders, then turned and winked over at Karen. 'Any chance of my favourite lady giving me supper tonight?'

Martha met his pleading expression with mock annoyance. 'I suppose I can fit you in,' she grumbled.

A little after seven, after checking Ellie was settled in bed with her favourite book, and with a half-promise to try, if she could, to pop back up and say goodnight after dinner, Karen made her way back downstairs.

Uncertain how formal the occasion would be, and as the heat of the day still lingered, she had decided on a simple cap-sleeved dress in soft khaki cotton. Her long hair cloaked her shoulders in one gleaming chestnut sweep.

At the foot of the stairs, she paused

for a moment. Pre-dinner drinks were taken in the main sitting room, she'd been told by Martha.

The sitting room door was slightly ajar and from the laughter escaping from it, she imagined Tony was being as entertaining as ever.

The small feeling of awkwardness gone, she opened the door. The first thing she noticed was Neil wasn't there.

She caught Caroline's eye and greeted her with a smile. Caroline was seated on one of the two plush burgundy sofas set side on to the fireplace. She raised her hand in welcome.

She looked particularly gorgeous tonight, Karen decided. Her hair was loose and the white sleeveless top she'd paired with powder blue evening trousers showed her tan off to perfection. Her green eyes were bright with laughter and, Karen noticed, now totally focused on Tony. She smiled to herself. Looked like he'd made another conquest.

'Ah, Karen,' Tony welcomed the moment she walked in. 'Looking just as beautiful as Caroline. I can see why Neil doesn't keep me up to date with what he's doing. Now can I get you a drink?'

'A small sherry, please,' she suggested, after greeting them all and ignoring his over the top flattery.

She joined Caroline on the sofa. Caroline then screened her words. 'I knew Neil had a stepbrother,' she whispered from behind her hand, 'but this is the first time I've met him.' They both watched Tony pick up the crystal decanter and pour the amber liquid into a delicate stemmed glass. 'Isn't he something?'

Karen grinned back at her. 'I suppose that's one way of putting it,' she agreed quietly.

'Sweet sherry for a sweet lady,' Tony said as he offered her the glass. Karen and Caroline both groaned in unison at his awful pun at which Tony played at being offended and rejoined Simon.

While Karen chatted to Caroline, in the back of her mind she wondered how long it would be before Neil made an appearance. Then she concluded he was probably spending some time with Ellie before coming down.

'Karen?' Caroline's gaze flickered over in Tony's direction again. 'D'you know if Tony has a regular girlfriend?' she whispered.

Karen shook her head. 'I know as much as you do.'

'Are you keen to know him better?' Caroline asked as Karen took a sip from her glass.

She almost choked on her sherry. She shook her head slightly. 'Fun though he seems to be,' she murmured, 'I don't think he's my type.'

'Good,' Caroline murmured. There was a glint of mischief in her eyes. 'That leaves the field open for me. Before this evening's over, I'm going to make it my business to find out if he's seriously attached. If not, I'll do something about it.'

And with that she tossed back her drink, leaving the rest to Karen's imagination.

Her speculation about the closeness of the two brothers' relationship crumbled the moment Neil entered the room. Immediately when his eyes lit upon Tony, she noticed the subtle set of his jaw and a steely glint in his gaze.

Puzzled, she glanced across to the fireplace to see if Tony realised Neil had joined them and what his reaction might be.

The moment his eyes lit upon Neil, Karen sensed a change in his manner. Despite the broad smile he threw him, they held a wariness which had not been evident before.

'Just been making sure everyone had a drink,' Tony said, 'while we were waiting for you to come down.'

'Appreciate it.' Neil responded with a slight nod of his head before helping himself to a whisky and soda. Then he glanced around at the others. 'Sorry for the delay,' he apologised after he had joined the group. 'Thanks to Karen . . .'

Her heart skipped a beat as he focused on her. To her discomfort, the same steely grey he had greeted his stepbrother with remained in his eyes.

What had she done? What was he about to say?

Then as the steel softened, she slowly released a breath.

' . . . Ellie hasn't enjoyed herself so much in a long time. I've just been hearing all the details, Karen, and been shown her pictures, too.'

Karen relaxed again, but once more sensed his smile had trouble forming. 'No thanks needed,' she responded. 'Believe me, I had just as much fun as Ellie.'

The circumstances of the motherless child and an overworked father formed in her mind and she felt deeply sympathetic.

Martha's arrival to announce dinner was about to be served, broke her introspection.

Neil waited while she and Caroline

got to their feet. 'Thanks again for Ellie,' he said as they made their way through to the dining room. 'You've made such a difference in the short time you've been here.'

She glanced up at him, once more very conscious of his presence. His hair gleamed darkly, still damp from the shower. 'It's my pleasure,' she said a little formally. 'I'm looking forward to tomorrow.'

At the long mahogany table, Karen swiftly manoeuvred herself to sit alongside Simon, directly across from Tony. A tension headache was beginning to niggle and right then she needed to put some space between herself and Tony's extroverted personality.

Caroline looked particularly pleased when Tony pulled out a chair for her then took the one alongside for himself. Neil took his place at the head of the table. Immediately he mentioned something to Caroline and Simon about their work.

'Next time I shall insist you sit next

to me,' Tony murmured. Karen glanced up to see his gaze flickering over from her across the table. She threw a glance at Caroline but doubted she or anyone else had heard what he had said.

While the others talked shop Martha began to serve watercress soup.

Tony Brookes was a serial flirt, she told herself, and as long as she kept that in mind she knew there was no danger of falling for him.

But she played the game and gave him the smile she knew he was hoping for. 'Will there be a next time,' she said, her eyes alight with playful provocation. Then all at once she sensed Neil's gaze upon her.

When she glanced up the table and met the coldness in his grey eyes. From his expression she had the feeling he had heard every word of Tony's, and her challenge, and did not approve.

She tried to indicate with a look it was just a little fun, not meant to be taken any further. But this had no effect.

His expression didn't alter as their eyes remained locked together for a moment longer. Then he turned his attention back to Caroline and Simon.

With a subdued word of thanks to Martha, Karen picked up her spoon. Why couldn't Neil lighten up a little?

A light pressure on her foot made her start. She drew her feet back under her chair and shot Tony a look of disapproval.

He wasn't fazed in the least. 'Oh yes,' he grinned. 'There will most definitely be a next time. Believe me.'

Knowing she could do nothing to prevent Tony's visits to the house, she determined she would do her best to ensure the seating plan remained as it was.

She smiled to herself. She was sure Caroline would be only too happy with that.

Tony turned his attention to the others and raised his voice. 'Come on, Neil. If you're going to talk business you should tell Karen and I more about all this buried treasure you're hoping to find.'

Rather than back Tony up, with a heavy heart Karen concentrated on her soup. She did not want to meet the same look of disapproval she was bound to get from Neil.

'Treasure in the sense you mean, Tony, is rare to come by,' she heard him reply.

'But if this should turn out to be a high status villa,' Simon joined in eagerly, 'and it's looking very much like it could be, who's to say what's . . . ' he tailed off. Karen glanced up and noticed the censorious look Neil was giving him.

Something had certainly altered Neil's mood since he'd welcomed her that morning.

Simon shrugged. 'It's been known before,' he muttered and picked up his spoon.

'You're right, Simon,' Caroline added supportively. 'The mosaic floor we're uncovering holds a lot of promise.'

'True enough,' Neil agreed, 'but let's

not jump the gun.' With that he turned his attention to his stepbrother. 'Enough of our work. Let's hear instead about the latest corner of the world you've been flying to.'

And then along with everyone else around the table, Karen listened to Tony's entertaining experiences in Australia and the Far East.

When they eventually finished Martha's delicious summer pudding served with crème fraiche they went back to the sitting room for coffee.

Everything was laid out and they each helped themselves, the men waiting until Caroline and Karen had poured.

'Let's take the sofa again,' Caroline suggested. 'There's more than enough room for three.'

Knowing what she was hinting at, Karen agreed but chose the space nearest to the broad arm. She did not want to give Neil a reason, however, unjustified, to produce more dark looks, if Tony sat beside her.

Caroline relaxed alongside. 'It's good

to have another woman to talk to,' she said, in between sips of coffee. 'Conversation tends to become focused on the one subject with just Neil and Simon for company. Work,' she grimaced, 'when sometimes I'd like to talk about girls' things. So let's swap life stories, shall we? Shall I go first?'

As Karen agreed to Caroline's suggestion she was still very much aware of Neil's presence. While Caroline chatted, Simon and Tony picked up a conversation.

Neil was the last to serve himself. When he picked up his cup and saucer and walked over to where she was sitting, for some inexplicable reason she felt her heart quicken.

'Karen,' he began. She looked up at him, unsure of what to expect. 'Caroline and Simon were well used to my routine of getting down to writing up my report after dinner, but I can't remember if I mentioned this to you yesterday.'

'Yes, you did,' she confirmed. 'Will

you be saying goodnight to Ellie first? Only I'd half-promised I'd pop my head around her door after we'd eaten. Too many interruptions might not be such a good idea.'

Approval softened his gaze and her spirits rose. 'I said goodnight to her before I came down.' Then his mouth curved a little. 'I don't see a problem with you doing the same.'

'Thank you.'

'And now if you'll all excuse me,' he addressed everybody, 'I have some writing to do.'

From start to finish, Karen's first meal at Mile End had been something of a roller-coaster ride as she'd tried to keep her mind on the table conversation and parry Tony's attempts at flirting with both herself and Caroline.

It had all been a little harmless fun, nothing else. She had the feeling Tony realised from her reactions that he had met his match but was still enjoying himself.

Simon was the next to leave.

'Seeing Janine again?' Caroline asked after he had placed his cup and saucer on the tray and said he was going out. 'It must be love,' she teased.

'Is that right,' he said with a satisfied smile.

'Well, you're looking very pleased with yourself and you've seen her almost every night for about the past month. Seems like you're really keen,' she continued to probe.

Simon's smile widened. 'I'll keep you posted. See you tomorrow.'

'Well, ladies,' Tony flashed a satisfied look at the two women after Simon had left, 'I can't believe my luck.'

'I'm afraid I'll have to be excused, too.' Karen got up from the sofa. 'I'm off to see Ellie.'

Karen caught the wink and the pleased look Caroline was giving her.

'Looks like it's just the two of us,' she heard Tony say as she closed the door. 'So how d'you think we should spend what's left of the evening?'

Chuckling to herself, Karen hurried

upstairs, convinced he didn't know what he was letting himself in for.

Caroline certainly had an interesting life. Travelling to several countries for both work and pleasure. And as for her boyfriends, Karen had lost count by the time Caroline brought her up to date with the one she'd been seeing before coming here. Vivacious was her middle name.

Long after checking on a sleepy Ellie, back in her own room propped up against her pillows, Karen put down the book she'd been reading. How could she concentrate when concern about Neil's attitude towards her was foremost in her mind.

This evening, for reasons she couldn't fathom, he'd been so very cool towards her, showing a preoccupied manner whenever she had participated in the general conversation, yet sharply focusing on whatever anyone else said.

Was he regretting his decision to have her there?

But that couldn't be the case, surely? She argued with herself. Not when he appeared to be so pleased with how she was caring for Ellie.

Perhaps she was over tired and it was just her imagination. After all his workload must be weighing heavily on him.

She glanced at her travel clock, surprised to see it was almost midnight. So much for an early night, she grimaced.

Smothering a yawn, she flattened her pillows then switched off her bedside lamp. Moments later, snuggled down under the covers, she fell into a restless sleep.

What woke her later, she wasn't sure. A heavy-eyed glance at the clock told her it was almost one forty-five.

She groaned and turned over. The next moment she heard a thud. Immediately, her eyes snapped open and she was wide awake.

In the partial light of the early hours she glanced around the shadowed room a little uneasily. But silence now hung heavily. Then the prolonged strangled shriek of a barn owl made her heart skip a beat.

She shot a wary look in the direction

of the window. The bird sounded so close to the house. She gave an involuntary gasp when the curtains were suddenly swept up from the windows and billowed into the room. For one nervous moment she thought the bird was flying in.

As the curtains continued to flutter she then saw what had woken her. One of the casement stays had slipped its hold and the window was swinging back and forth, banging against the frame.

Relieved it was only that, she scrambled out of bed and hurried across the room, eager to secure it before the noise woke anyone else.

As she leaned forward and grasped the curved brass handle, it was almost snatched from her hand by the force of the wind. She struggled for a moment or two until she was finally able to secure it again on the stay.

She shivered as she glanced out into the darkness of the stormy night which was such a contrast to a hot day they'd enjoyed.

High above her head, dark cloud formations scudded across the sky, intermittently plunging the landscape into a deeper darkness before the full moon reappeared and cast its silver light on the sleeping countryside.

Feeling she had the world to herself, she remained by the window a moment longer and looked at the now colourless shapes of the garden shrubs and the nearby fields.

Then the moon escaped the clouds again and bathed the night scene in a brighter light. Growing a little colder, she decided to close the window completely in case it became free again.

As she raised her hand, a sudden movement in the corner of her eye sent her heart crashing against her ribs. Straining her eyes at the shadowy scene below, there appeared to be someone moving about in the field where Neil, Simon and Caroline had been working.

5

Putting the previous night's experience down to troubled sleep after the moon's reappearance revealed an empty landscape, next morning Karen checked Ellie's room on her way down to breakfast. Ellie was nowhere to be seen.

With a pang of guilt for not hearing her alarm, she hurried down the stairs and made her way into the kitchen.

Met by a lively atmosphere and the delicious aroma of breakfast cooking, Karen realised just how hungry she felt.

She was also aware of a small flicker of disappointment when she saw Neil was not at the table with Ellie, Caroline and Simon, who were all enjoying breakfast, while Martha was busy grilling bacon.

But of course, she recalled, he began work at six o'clock.

'Morning, everyone,' Karen greeted, giving Ellie a special smile. Ellie was still wearing the pink polka dot pyjamas she had picked to wear the night before.

'Morning, Karen,' Martha responded, along with the others before turning back to the rashers of bacon she was grilling. 'Fruit juice in the fridge,' she called. 'Cereal on the counter if you'd like some. Just help yourself. This will be ready in a few minutes.'

'Thanks, Martha. Juice will be fine but I'll skip the cereal if you don't mind. Sorry I'm a bit late,' she apologised to everyone. 'I woke in the night then when I finally got back to sleep, I missed my alarm.'

'Are you a light sleeper?' Simon asked when she pulled out the chair next to Ellie. 'That must be a pain.' His frown of concern touched her.

'No, not usually,' she shook her head then sipped the chilled fresh orange juice. 'It was probably the mixture of different surroundings, strange bed, that sort of thing.'

'I find that, too.' Caroline joined in. 'But with all this fresh country air and the digging we've been doing lately, I've been going out like a light as soon as my head touches the pillow.'

'Well there's your answer,' Simon said. 'You'll have to join us on the site.'

'Karen can't,' Ellie piped up at once. 'She'll be busy with me and we'll be doing more exciting things.'

'Well is that so,' Simon rolled his eyes at Ellie, to the general amusement around the table. 'Can I come and join you then?'

Ellie shook her head. 'We'll be doing girls things' and Dad needs you more and Caroline.'

'So he does,' Simon nodded.

'Nice try, Simon,' Caroline chuckled. 'It's back to the site for us.' She nudged Simon's arm then moved her chair back and got up from the table. 'C'mon. Neil is putting us to shame.'

As Simon got to his feet, Martha came bustling over with another toast rack in one hand a huge plate of cooked breakfast in the other. 'There's plenty more,' she said as she placed them down in front of Karen. 'There you are, dear. This will build you up for the day.'

'See you later, folks,' Simon called as they disappeared out through the back door.

'Simon's funny,' Ellie grinned. 'He makes me laugh. 'Specially when Caroline bosses him around.'

'He makes me laugh, too.' Karen agreed, with a smile. 'Caroline's doing a good job. Now what shall we do today? Swimming baths, the zoo or a picnic in the woods?'

'Swimming,' Ellie clapped her hands with excitement. 'It's ages since Dad took me.'

As Karen finished breakfast, she decided she would need to take a long walk before she slipped into the water at the Leisure Centre.

The day has passed far too quickly, she reflected later when she drove back to Mile End. She glanced down at Ellie alongside her in the passenger seat. She seemed to be having trouble keeping her eyes open.

She's a bundle of energy, Karen thought with growing affection, but after all they'd done today, even she was feeling in need of a shower to liven her mind up again.

As soon as she pulled up outside the house, Ellie came to like a shot. She released her seatbelt the moment Karen switched off the engine then turned to her with happy anticipation. 'Let's go find Dad,' she enthused. 'I want to tell what we've done today.'

Karen glanced at her watch. It had just turned four o'clock. Mindful she was there to give Neil as much free time as she could to enable him to get on with his work, she knew a little diplomacy was needed.

'That's a good idea, Ellie. But I think first of all we should take our swimming costumes into the kitchen and rinse them. Then we can hang them outside to dry while it's still sunny.'

Ellie considered this for a moment.

'OK,' she agreed. 'And then we'll find Dad.'

After they had had fun rinsing out their costumes in the utility room and mopping up the resulting water spills, Karen managed to stretch the time out a little further by suggesting Ellie tell Martha all they'd done that day. Over a glass of milk and one of Martha's freshly-baked scones, Ellie went into great detail.

A little later when Ellie flung herself at her father as Neil greeted them down on the site, Karen found herself feeling the same involuntary leap of her heart as when she'd first met him.

'Ellie wanted to tell you what we've done today,' she said, 'I hope we're not holding you up,' she added quietly.

'Not at all. We're just finishing off.' There was an unexpected warmth in his grey eyes she welcomed. 'We've had a good day.' He gestured with his hand towards the ground and Karen could see yesterday's trench was extended considerably. 'Cleared a good section, as you can see.'

'Any further finds?' she asked, then wondered if she'd said the right thing. If they hadn't she guessed Neil would be feeling a sense of frustration.

'One or two,' he nodded. 'It's still looking favourable.'

Dinner that evening, Karen considered, as she listened to Neil discuss his ideas for the next day, was a much quieter affair without Tony's outgoing presence.

Neil's manner was far more relaxed. While he discussed the site, he continued to bring her into the conversation with a natural ease that had her feeling she had known him a lot longer than a mere few days. The occasional smile he sent in her direction brought a sense of breathlessness she'd not known before.

'Sorry for talking shop,' he said as they finished dessert. 'We must have bored you rigid. Put a group of archaeologists together and we tend to get carried away.'

'I wasn't bored in the least,' she exclaimed with feeling. 'It's been absolutely riveting. I'd never realised how fascinating archaeology could be. I've learned a lot this evening.'

Was she imagining his look of approval, she wondered, or was he really flattered by what she'd said?

'If that's the case we should soon have another pair of hands to help us,' Simon teased.

'Not if Ellie has anything to do with it,' Karen chuckled. 'Remember what she said at breakfast.'

Outside in the hall, the ringing of the telephone interrupted the mood around the table. Neil got to his feet. 'Excuse me. I'll just get that.'

He returned in a matter of moments and Karen could see at once his manner had changed. 'Tony's on the line,' he announced. Karen saw Caroline's eyes light up. 'You'd better have a word with him, Karen.'

Immediately her heart sank. 'Me?'

'Yes. Apparently he's promised Ellie and yourself a trip in his plane.' The censorious look he flashed her had her feeling she should have mentioned this to him the day of Tony's visit.

'It was a promise I believe he made last time he was staying with your mother and stepfather,' she responded coolly, determined to let him know she was not keeping anything back. 'Ellie reminded him when he called the other day. He said he would talk to you about it.'

Neil's expression lightened a little. 'Oh, I see. Must have slipped his mind,' he muttered. 'I've no objections to Ellie going if you would like to take her. Despite his devil may care attitude to most things, Tony is an excellent pilot. He's holding on waiting for you to confirm which day suits.'

'Of course.' Karen got to her feet, aware of Caroline's disappointment.

She hurried through to the hall and picked up the receiver. Tony's lively response to her greeting was in sharp contrast to Neil's reaction.

'Well if tomorrow is all right with you,' Karen suggested, 'we could do it then. I'm sure Ellie can't wait.'

'Perfect, perfect.' Tony's pleasure was almost tangible. 'Right, I'll pick up my two favourite girls at ten o'clock tomorrow morning, then.'

Deep in thought she replaced the receiver then glanced up towards the dining room to see Neil's tall figure in the open doorway, cup of coffee in his hand. Her first thought was to wonder if he had been listening to her conversation.

'You've made the arrangements?'

'Yes, we've decided on tomorrow. Ellie's so excited about the flight I can't see any point in putting him off.'

With that Neil raised a quizzical brow. 'Sounds like you're not exactly enthralled by the prospect.'

If she was true to herself she would have admitted this was so. While taking a flight in a light aircraft would be a novelty, a day spent with Tony was bound to be hard work. But a contrary side of her she'd not known before, had her saying, 'Oh, no you mustn't think that. I'm looking forward to it just as much as Ellie.'

He gave her a guarded look. 'That's fine then,' he muttered. 'I'll be in my study for the rest of the evening. Enjoy tomorrow.'

'Goodnight, Neil and thank you.' She forced a smile, then knowing it was more than likely he would be down on the site by the time she came down to breakfast, said, 'I'm sure Ellie will have lots to tell you when we get back.'

'Yes I'm sure she will.' He walked across to the door facing the dining room. After he'd opened it he paused and looked at her. 'As no doubt you will, too.'

'Oh, I shall,' she confirmed with false brightness. 'I'm bound to have something to add. That's if you're prepared to listen.' The thought was out before she realised it. 'I mean, of course,' she back-tracked quickly, 'that you have far more important things to do.'

She held her breath while she waited for his response.

His hand remained on the doorknob, a frown marked his brow. 'That could depend on how your day goes, Karen,' he responded enigmatically. And with that he opened his study door and disappeared inside.

Up in her room, Karen stood at the open window and gazed with unseeing eyes into the distance. She reflected on every conversation she and Neil had had since she'd arrived at Mile End and still couldn't draw any conclusions.

She walked over to the bedside table, picked up her mobile and keyed in her friend, Jenny's, number.

Next morning Karen woke early to what promised to be another hot day. A little later, dressed in a cool blue top and navy cropped pants, she hurried down to the first floor landing to see this time Ellie's bedroom door was closed.

'Today is going to be an extra special one,' she announced after a tousle-headed Ellie had responded to her knock and pushed herself up from under her duvet when Karen popped her head around the door.

She felt a pang of guilt for waking her but a glance at Ellie's bedside clock showed it was almost an hour beyond the time Neil told her she usually woke. She smiled to herself. Yesterday's trip to the swimming baths had obviously tired her out.

'Are we going swimming again?' Ellie asked, rubbing her eyes.

'Better than that,' Karen enthused. She sat down on the bed. 'But before I tell you I want you to get washed then I'll brush your hair and put it up in a pony tail.' Her expression teased. 'You won't want it flying,' she emphasised, 'all over your face, where we're going.'

During the long drive to the airfield in Tony's four-by-four, he kept Ellie entertained with tales of his flying. And not to put a damper on the mood, Karen had laughed in the right places when he had gone into flirt mode.

'We can have lunch there later,' Tony gestured with a nod at the country inn they were just passing. 'Providing a certain person feels like eating,' he teased, 'after her flight.'

'D'you mean me, Uncle Tony?' Ellie's hesitant question came from the back seat.

'Of course not, Ellie.' Karen shot Tony a warning glance. Talk like that could be off-putting for a child. Abashed he gave her a wry look. 'Uncle Tony is talking about me. I told him earlier I've not flown many times before.'

When Tony drove through the entrance to the airfield, Karen looked around with interest at the large, pitched-roofed hangars and what she took to be the control tower.

'Right, ladies,' Tony said, pulling into a space in the area set aside for parking. 'Just need to make a few checks with the staff then we'll be away.'

A short while later while they were still admiring some of the small planes, Tony rejoined them. 'OK, we're logged in,' he said. 'Plane's over there. Can you see, Ellie?' He pointed up ahead. 'The blue and white one.'

'It's going to be a great adventure.' Karen reassured Ellie as she felt her small hand tighten within her own and wondered for all her confidence if she was now feeling a little nervous. 'You'll have all kinds of things to tell your dad. I've remembered my camera so you can take some pictures if you like.'

In their seats behind Tony, Ellie still kept a tight grip on Karen's hand as the blue and white four-seater Cessna taxied on to the runway and quickly gathered speed. Then they took to the air and the countryside opened up below them.

Any sense of anxiety Ellie had been feeling was soon lost as Karen pointed out the various landmarks to her. The plane was the high winged type so their view was unrestricted.

'How about flying over your house, Ellie?' Tony suggested. 'We'll probably see your dad and Simon and Caroline working in the field.'

'Yes, please.' Ellie's delight was palpable.

Eagerly, Ellie peered out of the small window, ready to be the first to spot her father. 'Look,' she cried out, 'there he is.'

'So I take it you enjoyed yourself,' Tony said to Karen later after they were back on solid ground and were walking back to where they were parked.

'Very much,' she said, wondering if she was the only one who felt a little light-headed after the experience. 'We couldn't have picked a more perfect day, could we?' she added. 'Flying over the Snowdon range, the Cheshire plain and the Wirral peninsula was absolutely breathtaking.'

'I liked being up in the blue sky and the sun glittering on the sea and the tiny ships we saw,' Ellie chipped in. 'And seeing Dad, of course.'

'Want to open up, Ellie?' Tony asked offering his key fob.

Ellie slipped her hand from Karen's and took the fob off him. Then she ran ahead to the four-by-four.

'Yes, thanks again, Tony,' Karen added as she watched Ellie go. 'It was a wonderful experience.'

He broke into a grin. 'Well in that case, we must do it again. But next time, what d'you say to just the two of us?'

Karen gave him a small smile. 'I'm not sure. I'm fully occupied with Ellie. What about Caroline, though?'

'Ah, sweet Caroline. But she's such a busy lady. Neil seems to be taking up all her time.'

'Not during the evenings, surely?' Karen questioned. 'He's closeted in his study every night after dinner.'

'Is that so,' Tony reflected. 'You sound a little put out by that.'

Heat flooded her cheeks. 'Not at all,' she dismissed quickly, reluctant to meet his eyes. 'I'm there purely for Ellie's sake.'

She hoped she'd sounded convincing enough. Tony's conjecture had disturbed her. Surely she wasn't wearing her heart on her sleeve?

'Well, that's good to hear.' He flashed her a smile. 'Looks like I could be in with a chance after all.' His smile did nothing for her. 'That's it, Ellie,' he called as the locking system was released.

I doubt it, Karen said to herself as she checked Ellie's seat belt was secure before she climbed in alongside Tony.

6

'Dad, we're back,' Ellie began to call when she reached halfway down the garden. Arriving home, she couldn't wait to see her father to tell him about the flight.

Watching her small figure disappear through the gap in the hedge and into the field beyond, Karen increased her pace. Alongside, Tony did the same. But by the time they reached the hedge, she could see Ellie was already standing on the edge of the trench where Neil was working.

Caroline was crouched at the far end busy scraping back the surface soil. Simon was halfway between the two.

'Ah, there's Caroline,' Tony said. 'I'll think I'll have a word. See if she's doing anything tonight.' He threw Karen a wry look.

Karen smiled to herself. Her theory

about Tony looked like being the right one. Then as she watched Neil greet his daughter with affection she found the familiar lump back in her throat.

'You saw us, Dad?' Ellie's voice and her excitement carried on the breeze.

'Yes, we all did. Didn't you see us wave back to you?'

'Yes,' Ellie gasped, still bubbling. 'You all looked like tiny people. It was great, honestly,' she enthused, her eyes like saucers, her body animated. 'We saw the mountains and the sea. And Karen let me take lots of photos with her camera.' She shot round to see if Karen had arrived. 'Didn't you, Karen?'

Neil looked over to where she and Tony were making their way across the field towards them.

When she saw the smile fade from his lips, her mood plummeted. Was that his reaction to herself, she wondered, or was it something to do with Tony and the edge there still seemed to be between them.

Then she wondered if she was

making too much of it when his expression lightened again. He stepped out of the trench to greet them.

'Karen, Tony. It's good to see you're all back.'

She couldn't decide whether he really meant it or was just being polite. To her surprise, he offered his hand to his stepbrother. 'Thanks for that, Tony. I think you've just about topped Ellie's holiday today.'

'Anytime,' Tony responded, giving Neil's hand a firm shake although, Karen noticed, he seemed a little thrown by his gesture. 'We could always do it another time when you're not so busy. Make it a foursome.'

'Oh, can we dad?' Ellie pleaded. 'I wanted you to come today.'

Neil smiled down at his daughter who now clung to his side, her face aglow. 'Of course. As soon as Uncle Tony and I both have a free day that suits us both, we'll do it.'

'Consider it done,' Tony said. 'Now will you excuse me. I'm just going to have a word with Caroline.'

Maybe Caroline would be the fourth person, this time Karen considered.

'Is that a promise, Dad?' Ellie asked as Tony wandered off.

'It most certainly is,' Neil assured her.

When he turned back to Karen his grey eyes were warm with laughter. Her heart picked up a pace when the warmth remained. 'You'll have to come, too,' he said, his tone quietly insistent.

'Of course Karen will,' Ellie emphasised before she could voice her thoughts that Caroline might be invited instead.

Ellie took hold of her hand. 'We're going somewhere else tomorrow, aren't we? To see your friend, Jenny, and I'm going to meet Lottie.'

Neil raised a brow. 'Jenny, I remember, but who's Lottie?'

He'd remembered her telling him about Jenny? With all he had to think about at the moment, Karen considered. She felt flattered.

'Lottie's Jenny's niece,' Ellie emphasised, as if her father should know this already. 'Karen said she's almost eight, too, and she's got blonde hair but she's not as tall as me and she goes to the village school.'

'That's right,' Karen confirmed with some amusement.

'Well, I can't keep up with your hectic lifestyle, Ellie Oldson,' Neil complained with mock protest.

'I rang Jenny last night,' Karen explained over Ellie's giggling. 'We arranged it then.'

'I hope she's feeling better.' The look was there again. Sincerity and friendliness and her spirits soared.

'She's getting there,' she said, quietly overcoming an unexpected breathlessness, 'but she still has to rest her ankle most of the time . . . Lottie is just as bubbly as Ellie. I'm sure they'll get on well together.'

Neil nodded his approval then gave Ellie his attention. 'Sounds like you're going to have another great day out.'

'Neil,' Simon's sudden call was a distraction. 'Can you come and take a look at this?'

The urgency of his tone ended Neil's and Karen's conversation. It alerted Caroline and Tony, too.

'Back in a minute,' Neil said. He dropped back into the trench and strode over to Simon. As far as Karen could see, Simon was still carefully scraping the soil as Neil crouched down beside him . . . 'What d'you think you've got?' Neil asked.

'Could be a coin. I think it could be gold.'

Caroline hurried over to see what he had.

'Looks like things are hotting up,' Tony said as he rejoined Karen and Ellie.

A sense of anticipation hung in the air as Neil carefully helped extract something from the earth. 'Looks like you're right,' he exclaimed. 'It's definitely a Roman coin.'

Karen wondered if everyone else felt

the same impatience as Neil carefully rubbed the coin with this thumb.

Then he grinned at his two colleagues. 'It is gold. Well done, Simon.'

Karen's heart beat a little faster at the implication of what Neil had just said.

'Vespasian?' she heard Caroline suggest.

'Looks very much like him,' Neil agreed happily.

'We want to see, Dad,' Ellie cried out eagerly, echoing Karen's thoughts.

With a great deal of satisfaction in his expression, Neil brought the coin over.

'Here you are, Ellie. Hold out your hand.' Her placed the coin on her palm. Karen and Tony peered at it too. 'That is the Emperor Vespasian. He came to Britain during the time of the Roman invasion as a legionary commander and then years later was crowned Emperor.'

Karen gazed at the imprint of a man's head decorated with a garland of laurel leaves imprinted clearly on the coin. 'See there,' Neil pointed out, 'his name is stamped around the edge of the coin. And on the back,' he turned it over, 'is the figure of a bull.'

Behind him, Caroline and Simon were eagerly clearing the earth in the same spot. 'Neil,' Simon called, his voice filled with the same expectancy. 'I think we have,' he paused while he did a little more careful scraping, 'another.'

To everyone's delight, another eight coins were unearthed in a matter of minutes.

'You've been proved right, Neil,' Caroline exclaimed after Neil had decided they'd exhausted that particular space. 'I'm so pleased. The extra funding has to be guaranteed now.'

Neil was cautiously optimistic. 'Let's not get too carried away,' he said, but Karen could see the satisfaction he was feeling. He held up the shallow wooden box containing the coins. 'I've still got to back these up.'

'You will.' Simon beamed at everyone. 'Although I still can't believe what we've got.'

'Well I can,' Tony exclaimed. 'Buried treasure. This calls for champagne.'

Later, after Neil had carefully cleaned the coins and declared them to be in mint condition, he happily bowed to pressure and arranged them in a small cloth lined box.

He also agreed, Karen was convinced mainly in recognition of Simon's good work, that they could be given the centre place on the dining table that night.

'But just for tonight,' he insisted. 'After which they will be locked away for safekeeping in my desk drawer.'

'Are they very valuable?' Karen asked him somewhat in awe of their history while they were having dinner.

'Because of their condition, yes they are,' Neil confirmed. 'I'm pretty certain some collectors would give around three thousand pounds for each of these coins.'

While her eyes widened at the price, Tony's impressed whistle pierced the momentary silence around the table. 'You're kidding me?' he exclaimed.

Neil shook his head. 'No. Some

Roman artefacts, because of their rarity or condition, can fetch very high prices. That's why I want no publicity about our work . . . especially after today's finds.'

'No, of course not,' general agreement went round the table.

'Unfortunately the site has very easy access to anyone with the wrong motives. Hopefully, the funding will go some way into making it more secure.' He looked at them each in turn. 'In the meantime, please remember what I've said.'

After the meal was over, Karen suppressed a smile at Caroline's immediate acceptance when Tony suggested they take a drive into Chester.

Simon was also eager to go and see Janine. Even though Karen had the feeling he was itching to impress her, he, Caroline and Tony complied when Neil reminded them it was imperative they did not discuss the coins in public, nor mention the find to anyone else.

'So you had a good time today?' Neil

said when he and Karen were alone.

She was still surprised he'd taken time out to join her on the sofa instead of taking his coffee through to the study and it took a moment for his question to sink in.

'Of course. It was absolutely wonderful,' she responded, her eyes in bright contrast to Neil's suddenly shadowed gaze. 'I've never experienced anything like it before. I'm so pleased your predictions about the site are gaining strength now you have the coins.'

'The coins?' he echoed, his features relaxed again. 'No, you misunderstand. I was talking about the flight. Your day with Tony.'

Karen came down to earth again. Everyone's pleasure, Neil's in particular, over the discovery still remained foremost in her mind.

'Oh that,' she said, gathering her thoughts together. 'Er, yes . . . yes I did. It was lovely to see how much Ellie enjoyed herself. She was almost buzzing with excitement by the time we landed.'

Neil nodded. 'I can imagine. I'm only sorry I wasn't there to witness her first flight in a light aircraft.'

Glancing at him, Karen sensed he was regretting the time he missed with his daughter. She gave him a smile of encouragement. 'But you did,' she said. 'Ellie gave a repeat performance when we got back, even more so I reckon, when she told you all about it.'

She felt a rush of pleasure to see he was heartened by this. 'I'll put the roll of film in the chemist's tomorrow. Then you'll have a clearer picture of what we saw.'

'It's clear Tony impressed you.'

His observation took her by surprise. She frowned as she set her cup and saucer down on the low table with more of a clatter than she'd intended.

'Sorry,' he apologised right away, when she looked back at him and he sensed her discomposure. 'I shouldn't have said that. Your private life is none of my business.'

Karen looked away. If only he knew

there was no other man she would rather be spending the evening with than him.

'There's no need for you to apologise,' she insisted quietly, forcing herself to meet his grey gaze once more. 'Thinking about it, yes I was impressed by our trip today, but it was purely over Tony's skill as a pilot, nothing more.'

For a moment silence fell between them. 'Then you don't object to him taking Caroline out for the evening?'

Karen's puzzlement deepened. Why should Neil be concerned with her feelings? Because any upset she was feeling could have a detrimental affect on Ellie. That's all, a small voice mocked.

She took this as a slight to her professionalism. 'Not in the least,' she said, her tone leaving no room for doubt.

Maybe, she told herself, she would be overstepping the mark by giving Neil her honest opinion of Tony, after all they were related, but she felt the need to say it and avoid any further misunderstanding.

'And I hope you don't mind me saying this, Neil, but as far as I'm concerned your stepbrother is an out-and-out flirt and I could never take him seriously.'

Something in his manner told her she hadn't put her foot in it at all. In fact he appeared visibly relaxed.

'Good,' he smiled. 'I'm pleased he hasn't pulled the wool over your eyes.' He paused for a moment and she sensed there was something on his mind.

'I think I should be frank,' he continued. 'Tony was something of a wild child when my mother and Gerald, his father, got together. Throughout his teens he caused them a good deal of distress getting into one scrape after another. Although that's a long time ago now. I, er . . . I've been concerned about the impression he might have made on you.'

His concern touched her and lifted

her heart. 'But what about Caroline?' Her thoughts were spoken before she realised it.

Neil's smile turned into a chuckle. 'Oh, Caroline. I've no worries there. I've know her for some years now and believe me where men are concerned she is more than able to take care of herself. Tony might find he's taken on more than he can handle.'

For some reason Karen suddenly felt affronted. Her eyes flashed. 'But he'd be able to handle me?'

The laughter died in Neil's eyes. He reached out and took her hand. Despite her annoyance with him a frisson of excitement raced down her spine. 'You have a gentle nature, Karen. I'm of the opinion you take things to heart. Tony is the love them and leave them kind. I wouldn't want you to get hurt,' he murmured. 'Despite all you've said.'

She swallowed again, her senses tingling from the warmth of his skin. 'I'd never consider Tony seriously,' she answered huskily.

Neil's mouth curved. 'I'm glad. Tony isn't always the life and soul of the party. He can be . . . well never mind. I think that's enough said about my stepbrother for one night.'

Then to her surprise, he raised her hand and brushed it with his lips. Wide-eyed she looked back at him.

'Just a thank you,' he smiled, 'for the wonderful job you're doing with Ellie. She hasn't been as happy as this in a long time.'

Disappointment washed over her. His gesture had been a thank you, that was all. She'd be a fool to think it could be anything more. She drew in an unsteady breath and forced a show of brightness. 'It's my pleasure,' she said. 'She's a lovely little girl.'

'Thank you.'

He released her hand and gave her a wry look. 'Much as I'd like to sit here and chat for as long as you want to, it's back to work for me, I'm afraid. After today's excitement I need to get the report finished as quickly as I can.'

He got to his feet. 'Once it's finalised, maybe we could spend more time together. What d'you say?' From her place on the sofa, Neil towered over her as he waited for her reply.

Time together? There was nothing she would like more. But the same small voice returned. It would only be while she was looking after Ellie. That was all. Nothing more.

'Yes. That would be nice,' she smiled up at him. 'There's still a lot on Ellie's list we haven't done yet.'

'Er, yes,' he hesitated, the thoughtful furrow she'd come to recognise was back in his brow then was gone again. 'Of course. Goodnight, Karen. I'll see you sometime tomorrow.'

'Goodnight, Neil.'

As she watched him leave the room she battled with her feelings. You are not falling in love with him, she told herself. It's a silly infatuation. That's all.

But later, propped up in bed, Neil's suggestion kept repeating over in her mind distracting her from the paperback she'd been trying to concentrate on for the past hour.

Then the carrying sound of tyres crunching on gravel coming from the front of the house was a further distraction. She glanced at her alarm. It had just turned ten o'clock. She frowned. A little early for the others to be back yet.

When the loud thud of only one door closing followed almost immediately, she guessed it was Simon. Caroline would have invited Tony in for a coffee.

She hoped there hadn't been a hitch in Simon's romance with Janine. It was clear to see as far as Simon was concerned, this was the real thing.

7

'So, tell me all about Ellie's father,' Jenny prompted impatiently. She was resting her bandaged ankle on a garden lounger. Karen was relaxing on a matching one alongside, enjoying the sun while watching Ellie and Lottie playing at the far end of the long garden. She was pleased the girls were getting on so well together.

She turned her head. 'There's not a lot to tell.'

'Come on, Karen,' Jenny insisted. 'It's like getting blood from a stone. When we talked the other night I got the feeling Professor Oldson had made an impact on your life.' Her brown eyes twinkled. 'A positive one, I hope.'

Thankful her dark glasses disguised the depth of her feelings, Karen shrugged casually. 'I'm enjoying being there, if that's what you mean.'

'No, I don't. Tell me more, for heaven's sake,' Jenny probed. 'His looks, his personality. That kind of thing. Is he attractive or not?'

'In a rugged kind of way,' Karen responded thoughtfully.

Jenny sighed. 'The best kind of all. So he's a widower in his mid-thirties, owns a country house, has a fascinating job.' She sighed again. 'Sounds a real catch. But you're going to ruin it all now by telling me there's a lady in his life?'

Someone else in his life?

The thought was devastating. 'As far as I know, there isn't,' she heard herself say, backing this up with the conviction with Ellie's open nature she was bound to have said something.

'So what are you doing about it?'

'Jenny,' Karen protested. 'I work for him.'

'So?'

'And I've only known him for little over a week.'

'What's that got to do with anything? You know at once whether you like a person or not and judging from his poppet of a daughter, I get the feeling he's quite something.'

'Well, maybe,' was all she would admit to. 'Anyway enough about my love life, or lack of it. How are you feeling?'

Jenny sighed. 'Frustrated more than anything. Still it has its compensations. As you can imagine Mum is spoiling me rotten. Waiting on me hand and foot . . . sprained foot,' she added drily. 'I still feel guilty about ruining your holiday, though. Having to cancel on the last minute. You must think I'm a real pain.'

Holiday, Karen reflected. It suddenly struck her that from the moment she'd met Neil, she hadn't given it another thought.

'Don't be ridiculous, Jen,' she protested. 'It was hardly your fault. I'm having a great time with Ellie. Neil's colleagues are great company, too. And would you believe his stepbrother is an airline pilot. He took us for a spin in his own light aircraft yesterday. Flew over your house, actually.'

'What! If I didn't need this cushion, I'd throw it at you. So,' Jenny's eyes twinkled, 'Simon who you mentioned the other night and this pilot uncle of Ellie's are either of them available?'

Karen laughed. 'Jenny you get worse the older you get.'

'Hopefully,' Jenny grinned.

* * *

'You really enjoyed yourself today, didn't you?' Karen said later as she and Ellie drove past Hartley's farm on the way back home.

Ellie nodded. 'I liked Lottie. I wanted to tell her about the treasure but I didn't 'cos Dad doesn't want us to yet, does he? He reminded me when he came up to say goodnight.'

Karen nodded. 'That's right, Ellie. He still has a lot of work to do before we can tell anyone else. It was very grown up of you not to tell Lottie about it.'

Ellie looked pleased with herself. 'Prob'ly I can tell her when the holidays are over. She said she'd be my best friend when I start at her school.'

Glancing at Ellie's happy face, Karen hoped Neil would decide to stay at Mile End. And not just for Ellie's sake, she admitted to herself. Right now she couldn't imagine life without knowing he was living nearby and having the opportunity of seeing him around the village.

As she slowed down and took the curve of the lane, the silver saloon car parked up ahead came as something of a surprise. Apart from the odd tractor or two, there was very little passing traffic at Mile End.

'Oh my daisy chain's broken.' Ellie's plaintive cry was a momentary distraction.

'Just leave it on your lap and I'll fix it once we're home,' Karen comforted then turned her attention back to the road ready to overtake the parked car.

As she indicated, the driver got out

and walked around to the front where he raised the bonnet.

When she drove past, she glimpsed a passenger. He had his head down and appeared to be reading something. Probably the handbook, she decided. She hoped they wouldn't have difficulty fixing it.

★　★　★

Karen woke early before her alarm went off. With the luxury of time on her hands, she lay in bed for a little while and reflected on the night before.

Several days had passed since Simon's discovery, but the excitement was still adding an extra buzz to the conversation around the table. Although she'd noticed there was something a little withdrawn about his manner and his initial enthusiasm over the coins now seemed laboured.

Definitely girlfriend trouble, she decided. It looked like she'd been right the other night, she reflected sadly, when he had returned early.

Happy in her developing relationship with Tony, Caroline's innocent probing about Simon's romance was met with curt responses.

Feeling she was wasting the day, she slipped out of bed and pulled on her dressing gown. It might be early, she mused, but not early enough to see Neil. He would be down on the site by now.

After padding across the landing to the bathroom, she took a long shower and planned the day. Ellie was keen to visit Chester again. Maybe they could do that.

Back in her room, her skin glowing, she decided to wear the blue summer skirt she'd recently bought and a plain cream top.

After slipping on her sandals she made her way down to the kitchen to have a coffee with Martha before she woke Ellie.

'Morning Mar — ' The words died on her lips when she was met by the scene of a tearful Martha sitting at the table, dabbing her eyes with a handkerchief.

Neil was in the chair alongside her, a comforting arm around her shoulder. His murmured strong tones appeared comforting although she couldn't quite make out his words exactly.

Her heart sank. Whatever could be wrong? Then her blood ran cold. It had nothing to do with the expected baby, surely?

'I'm sorry,' Karen began again, unsure of what to do or say. She took a step back. 'I'll come back later.'

'No, Karen. Don't go,' he said grimly. 'You can keep Martha company while I phone the police.'

Karen's eyes widened. 'The police?' she swallowed. Neil nodded. 'John's outside checking the gardens.' He got to his feet. 'Martha's had a bit of a shock. We were broken into last night. My desk drawer was forced open and the coins have been stolen.'

'Oh, no.' Karen's hand shot to her

mouth. 'I'll make some fresh tea,' Karen suggested, still trying to come to terms with what Neil had said but eager to be of some use.

By the time he returned to the kitchen, Martha was over her initial shock and was sipping hot tea. Karen had taken his place at the table. She looked up at him with anxious eyes.

'They'll be here shortly to interview us all,' he said. 'I've been upstairs and had a word with Simon. He'll be down soon. Karen would you mind waking Caroline. Explain what's happened. I've phoned Tony. He should be here within the hour. As he is the only other person to know about the coins, he'll have to be interviewed, too.'

'Of course.' She pushed back her chair. Concern for Neil had her wishing she could do more. 'What about Ellie?'

His expression tensed. 'I'll go up to her room now,' he said gruffly. 'I'm concerned about the effect this might have on her. Hopefully the police won't need to interview her but,' he shrugged, 'it will be impossible to keep it from her. She'll have to know what's happened.'

The police arrived a short time later and while the forensic team examined Neil's study, he suggested the interviews should take place in the sitting room.

At Karen's suggestion, Ellie was outside helping John in the vegetable garden. She'd been concerned when she'd seen her bubbly personality so much subdued when Neil had brought her down to the kitchen, even though he was holding her hand.

Martha was lying down in her room until it was her turn to be called.

'I just can't believe it,' Caroline said, not for the first time, while she, Karen and Simon sat around the table waiting to be called. Neil was with the Detective Inspector. 'Neil said the study window is smashed. That's how they got in. But I didn't hear a thing.'

Karen noticed Simon looked particularly hollow eyed and drawn. But having been the one who discovered the coins, she decided, he was bound to take the theft more personally.

'They have their methods, I suppose,' he muttered, staring at his hands.

'Caroline,' Neil called from the doorway. 'Would you like to come through first.'

Simon was next to be interviewed and came back looking just as troubled.

'Karen?'

Butterflies turned Karen's stomach over when Neil came through a few minutes later and called her name.

She gave him a strained smiled. 'My turn?'

He nodded then waited for her. 'I sat in on Caroline and Simon's interviews,' he said as they walked down the hall. 'The Inspector had no objection. Would you like me to sit in with you. It's your choice, of course.'

'Oh, please,' she breathed, eager to grab the support he was offering. 'I've never done anything like this before.'

Neil's mouth curved a little as he put

a reassuring hand on her shoulder. 'Don't worry. You'll be fine. Just answer the questions as best you can and if you do think of anything, particularly anything that might have struck you as being unusual, don't forget to mention it.'

The atmosphere in the sitting room could not be more different than the past few happy evenings, Karen reflected as Neil introduced her to Detective Inspector Barret and his assistant, Detective Constable Milne.

'Please, Miss Carmichael, take a seat.' The Inspector gestured to one of the easy chairs near the window. He waited until Karen had sat down, then took another. His assistant remained standing.

Neil perched on the end of the sofa nearest to them. Karen appreciated his brief smile of encouragement.

'Now what can you tell us, Miss Carmichael,' the Inspector began.

She swallowed. 'Very little, I'm afraid.'

Throughout her conversation with

the two policemen Neil's suggestion that anything at all could be of help stayed in her mind. As the interview drew to an end she remembered the car she'd seen parked in the lane.

'This is probably nothing,' she said, 'but a few days ago when Ellie and I were driving home, there was a car parked in the lane. A silver saloon. I can't remember the make, sorry.'

Within the short distance separating them, she sensed Neil's attention picking up.

'Why d'you think this should be of any significance,' DC Milne asked.

'Well it was rather unusual as we don't get a lot of traffic down here.'

'That's right,' Neil said, eagerly.

'But then,' she continued, not wanting to build his hopes up too much. 'The driver got out and raised the bonnet.' She shrugged. 'I think they must have broken down.'

'I don't suppose you noted the registration number, either,' DI Barret said.

Karen grimaced. 'Sorry.'

'Your daughter,' he addressed Neil, 'maybe she could help us with this?'

Neil's reluctance showed. 'I very much doubt it, but if you think it necessary.'

'Ellie's still in the garden,' Karen said. 'It might be better if you talked to her outside. It wouldn't be such a formal setting.'

The appreciation in Neil's eyes brought a warm glow to her face. 'Good idea. You come too, Karen.'

'Give me a brief run down what you'd done that day,' DI Barret instructed Karen as they left the house. 'It would help when I talk to the little girl.'

'Of course.' As they walked across the garden she quickly told him about their visit to Jenny.

They found Ellie carefully placing the new potatoes John was unearthing into an old trug. She gave the two detectives a wary look and slipped her hand into her father's while Neil explained who they were.

'Hello, Ellie. Those potatoes look good.'

Karen was relieved to see DI Barret's friendly manner had reassured her. 'Ellie,' he went on, 'can you remember the day you went to visit Karen's friend, Jenny?'

She nodded. 'Yes. I played with Lottie. It was good.'

'That's right. Karen's been telling me all about it. Now when you were almost home, did you see a car parked in the lane?'

Karen's heart went out to her when Ellie glanced anxiously up at her father. 'It's all right, sweetheart,' Neil said, 'you're doing fine.'

Then she felt a flicker of disappointment when Ellie slowly shook her head. 'I don't think so,' she said slowly. 'I was trying to fix my daisy chain. It had fallen off again.'

'That's all right, Ellie,' the detective said. 'You've done very well. You can go back to helping Mr Peters now.'

With Ellie out of hearing distance,

DC Milne turned to Karen. 'Pity there's no back up for what you say you saw.'

Troubled by his comment and his tone, Karen glanced at Neil for support. When she met his gaze she stiffened. A brief shadow of doubt steeled his eyes as he regarded her and a frown began to form on his brow.

The colour drained from her face then flooded back again. Surely he didn't think she had taken the coins and made up a story about a car in the lane to divert suspicion from herself?

A hollow feeling she'd never experienced before made her feel sick inside. She turned back to the detective. 'I can assure you there was a parked car,' she insisted coldly. 'You have my word for it.'

How she'd managed to charge off ahead of the three men, she didn't know. All that mattered was the need to flee from the horror of Neil's unspoken accusation.

When she reached the back kitchen

door, she fumbled with the handle. Her strength now seemed to have vanished from her arms as well as her legs.

'Karen, what's up?' Simon asked when she finally released the lock and burst into the kitchen. 'You look like you've seen a ghost.'

'Oh it wasn't a ghost,' she retorted angrily. 'Actually it was a silver saloon car.'

As Caroline and Simon exchanged puzzled looks, she was aware that Neil and the two detectives had joined them. 'Which some people find hard to believe.'

'Karen?' The concern in Caroline's voice almost brought her close to tears. 'Start at the beginning and maybe we can help.'

'A few days ago I saw a car parked in the lane,' she began to explain for the second time.

After she had finished, Simon nodded. 'Yes, it was there. I saw it, too.'

'You did!' Karen pulled out a chair. The feeling of relief was so enormous she had to sit down.

'I was in the paddock picking up some equipment I'd left there,' he explained to everyone. 'The view of the lane is uninterrupted there. The car Karen is talking about was parked a hundred yards or so away from the house.'

'It's a pity you didn't think to tell us about it earlier, sir,' Karen heard the DI say.

The ringing of the front door bell broke the strained atmosphere.

'That's probably my stepbrother,' Neil said to the DI. 'I'll take him through to the sitting room.'

'Thank you, sir.'

The two policemen followed Neil out of the kitchen.

'Right,' said Caroline. 'Simon and I are off to the site. Hopefully to take our mind off things,' she gave Karen a rueful smile.

'I need some air, too.' Karen got up with them. 'I think I'll sit in the garden for a while.'

She followed Caroline and Simon through the back door and chose one of the garden benches.

Leaning back, she raised her face and closed her eyes to the heat of the sun. She needed space to clear her head and come to terms with the fact that Neil had doubted her story.

A bone-aching weariness swept over her. How could he consider her to be a thief? Because you're someone he's known for a very short time, a small voice mocked. He took you on trust and for a moment back there he doubted it.

And if Simon hadn't backed me up, she mused, he would still be doubting me now. To remain here now was impossible. The sooner she was packed and gone, the better.

'Karen?' She froze, stiffening with tension when she heard Neil's voice nearby. 'I've been looking for you.'

'You have? Why's that?' Of course she knew why, she just wanted him to come out and say what he'd been thinking.

So why, she asked herself, couldn't she face him? After all she'd been vindicated. She had nothing to hide. Only the hurt, she told herself. And it wouldn't do to show Neil how susceptible she was to him.

'We need to talk. Mind if I join you?'

She quickly blinked back the sting of hot tears and pulled herself together. She shrugged and avoided a direct answer. Instead she swallowed hard and asked, 'Is it to do with Ellie?'

She hoped she sounded far more confident than she was feeling. He moved towards her and she saw for the first time how strained he was looking. 'Indirectly. I was concerned as to how you were feeling. You seemed a little upset before.'

Something inside her snapped. 'A little,' she mocked, her blue eyes flashing. 'I can assure you it was much more than a little. To have my integrity questioned by that oaf of a constable was frightening. Where would I stand now if Simon hadn't backed me up?

There was certainly no support coming from you.'

A dark stain of embarrassment coloured the line of his cheekbones. 'Karen, I . . . you mustn't think — '

'Why shouldn't I,' she cut in, 'when it was there in your eyes. I don't understand you, Neil. You trust me with the welfare of your daughter and yet just now you were set to believe I was somehow involved with the burglary. I don't know what you were thinking?'

'I don't know, either,' he said grimly. 'Things have been tough lately,' he tried another tack. 'The stress, the pressure to prove my gut feelings about the site is increasing daily — '

'Well I hope your gut feelings about the site are more accurate than the ones you've just had about me,' she swiftly interrupted again.

A heavy silence grew between them. Unable to stand the strain, she eventually broke it. 'I'd better go and pack my things,' she said wearily.

'Pack?' Neil flinched as if he'd been

hit. 'You can't leave,' he exclaimed. 'Ellie will be devastated.'

Not nearly as much as I would . . . as I'm feeling right now, she considered.

'Please, Karen. The burglary has been worrying enough for her. I don't think I could handle the upset of telling her you've gone.'

Of course she would. But it would be for Ellie. No-one else. Especially her doubting father.

She squared her shoulders. 'You're right, Neil,' she sighed. 'For Ellie's sake, I know I have to.'

8

'There it is, Ellie. Can you see it? That's the pretty clock I was telling you about.'

On their walk along the Roman walls surrounding the oldest part of the city, Karen pointed towards the gleaming cast iron structure of the famous domed Chester clock with its colourful ornate decoration of red, blue and gold, erected to celebrate Queen Victoria's Diamond Jubilee.

Ellie had asked to be taken to Chester for the day and Karen had readily agreed.

Since the burglary Ellie's sleep pattern had been disturbed and she was working on keeping her fully occupied in the hope of her having a better night's sleep. She was also avoiding Neil as much as she could.

As she watched Ellie peer down through the railings at the crowded

Eastgate Street full of browsing tourists and shoppers, she wondered how she had even thought of leaving.

She had become so fond of her she didn't like to think of the wrench it would be when her time there was over. The date was drawing closer far too rapidly.

'Karen, you have brought your camera?' Ellie asked.

'Yes, it's in my bag. Now how about I take a picture of you with the clock in the background. And then I'll ask someone if they will take a picture of us both together.'

An American couple who were also admiring the clock, were only too happy to photograph them together after Karen had asked. 'But you'll have to return the favour,' the young man joked which Karen did so with pleasure.

As she handed back his camera, a tall, dark-haired figure in the crowd below took her eye. Her heart turned over when she immediately thought it was Neil.

She frowned, sure she was seeing things. At this time of day he'd be on the site. But as he turned to cross the road she had a clearer view. It was him. She had no doubt.

What was he doing there? she wondered as he disappeared inside one of the shops. It must be something really important to take him away from his work.

'Karen, can we go to the shops now? I want to buy Dad a present.' Ellie's request broke her thoughts.

Karen's heart was touched. Despite the reassurance she had heard Neil give her since the theft, even Ellie had noticed the change in her father.

'So have you decided what you're going to buy?'

Ellie shook her head. 'I don't know what would be best.'

'How about a new pen?' Karen suggested after a few moments thought. 'He does a lot of writing, doesn't he?'

Ellie's eyes lit up. 'That is so cool. His favourite colour is red, so I'll get him a red one.'

Down in Eastgate Street as they walked hand in hand past the shop Karen had seen Neil enter, she glanced with some interest at the building. To see it was an antiques gallery specialising in Roman artefacts, came as some surprise.

She looked past the tastefully arranged window display of ancient pottery and glass and wondered if he was still inside the shop.

But the only customers she could see were an elderly couple and a young woman. Neil had already left.

Maybe her imagination had been playing tricks with her after all.

Back at Mile End Karen suggested Ellie wrote a little message on the tiny card she had been given to go with the gift-wrapped pen. 'You could leave it as a surprise on your dad's desk,' she suggested as she opened the front door.

Having seen Neil's car parked in its usual place in front of the house, she was confident he would be back down on the site.

Eager to do this, Ellie raced up the stairs while Karen went up to her own room to drop off some items she had bought.

Ellie was still carefully writing out her message when she rejoined her. Finally satisfied with her efforts, Ellie was keen to leave her gift on Neil's desk.

'Dad's going to have a great surprise, isn't he?' she grinned as she made a show of opening the study door quietly.

Then her face dropped. 'Dad!' she exclaimed, swiftly hiding the package behind her back. 'You're not supposed to be in here now.'

Karen didn't know who looked the more surprised. And if she didn't know better she would have said Neil's stunned expression was one of outright guilt.

Seated at his desk, he held an open box in his hand. As he stared back at them he appeared frozen in time.

Then immediately he went into action. As he snapped down the lid, Karen saw a brief flash of gold. Then he pushed it inside the drawer.

Unsettling thoughts began to form in her mind. She dismissed them instantly as Neil closed the drawer and got to his feet.

'Ellie, Karen. What are you doing here?' His smile was stiff and unnatural. 'But more importantly,' he gave Ellie a mock stern look, 'why am I not supposed to be in my own study?'

'It's a secret,' she pouted, full of disappointment that her plans had gone awry.

'Is that right.' His expression was wary as he glanced at Karen.

But would it be any different, she reasoned, the way things stood between them.

'Then perhaps Karen could tell me?'

She could see he was still unsure of how she would respond and it was difficult, she recognised, to fight her true feelings, as with continuing regret his eyes held hers.

'I can't,' she gave him a tentative smile. 'It's Ellie's secret.' Then as she

135

pictured again the bright red and gold patterned pen Ellie had bought for him, the unthinkable gained reason in her mind.

What was in the box Neil hadn't wanted them to see. As her mind raced in confusion two things kept coming to the fore. The stolen coins and Neil's visit to the antique shop. A chill ran down her spine.

Had he faked the burglary and had the coins all along? Was he in Chester having them valued?

Later, up in her room, her mind was in turmoil. For hours she had felt on automatic pilot, saying the right things in the right places when Ellie had given Neil his gift; acting out the expected responses to his surprise and Ellie's delight.

While all the time her mind was telling her she was mistaken. Neil would never have done such a thing. She had then excused herself and left Neil and Ellie in the study to spend some time together and gone to see

Martha in the kitchen.

Martha and John were off to see their daughter-in-law's baby son that evening. He had arrived the day before, ten days earlier than expected and Karen had readily agreed to step in and help cook dinner.

Caroline was spending the weekend with her sister. A taxi had arrived to take her to the station shortly after Karen and Ellie got back from Chester. Simon was out, too, having borrowed Neil's Land Rover again and wouldn't be returning until late Sunday night.

'Been invited up to meet his girl-friend's parents, I believe,' Martha said. 'Last minute thing. Looked a bit tense, he did. Poor thing,' Martha continued. 'Said they're quite a prominent family. I told him not to worry. When you get down to it, we're all just the same really, aren't we? Just people.'

Recalling Martha's philosophy, Karen's mood darkened. She could give her an argument about that. Some people turned out to be quite the opposite of what you believed them to be.

As she checked her appearance in the mirror, it struck her that what she had chosen to wear without any conscious decision suited her mood perfectly. A simply cut black top and black trousers. It was as if she was in mourning, she told herself, for something unobtainable . . . something lost forever.

She frowned at her reflection. It didn't help that tonight she and Neil would be dining alone. She could always confront him of course, but did she have the mental strength to deal with the consequences should she be proved right?

She frowned, doubting herself for a minute. Had she really seen what she'd thought. She called her mind back to Neil's guilty actions and her doubt died.

There was definitely something gold in the box. Something that had a circular edge, she was absolutely certain.

She recalled his words . . . collectors would pay up to three thousand pounds for each coin. Simon had discovered ten. It didn't take a genius to work out their value.

Was Neil using the sale of these as back-up in case he didn't get the funding? If he hadn't looked so flustered; been his usual assured self, she wouldn't be having these thoughts now. It was just not him. Something was definitely wrong.

She needed to talk to someone about it. Someone who knew him well. She was loathe to admit her suspicions to either Caroline or Simon. They would defend him to the last, she was sure. That left only one other person.

Tony.

They'd been stepbrothers since they were teenagers she remembered Neil telling her.

Mind made up, she punched in the number of his mobile, glad now he'd pressurised her into having it. On the fourth ring she was connected and she blurted out that she desperately needed his help.

'Of course, just spell it out,' came Tony's reassuring support.

She took a deep breath and told him of her suspicions.

'Tell me I'm being ridiculous, Tony,' she said, after he had listened in silence.

Now she had voiced her concerns she felt utterably miserable. They sounded ludicrous. 'Then we can just forget the whole matter. I'm thinking now as we speak that what I've told you is an insult to Neil's integrity.'

'Well,' Tony considered slowly, 'it does seem a bit off the wall, doesn't it? Tell you what, do absolutely nothing for the time being while I mull over what you've said.'

'OK then, I'll wait for your call. But please get back to me as soon as you've considered what's best to do. And you won't say anything about it to anyone else, will you?'

'Trust me, sweetheart. My lips are sealed.'

She could sense Tony's smile in his tone. She frowned. This wasn't a smiling matter.

After he ended the call, Karen checked her watch. It was time to prepare dinner. She braced herself to go down. The last thing she felt like doing right now was eating.

For once, silence hung in the kitchen as she busied herself taking the chicken out of the oven and transferring it on to a serving plate.

It had been Neil's suggestion that they eat in there as it was just the two of them tonight.

She almost dropped the serving dish she was holding when the phone in the hall began to ring, stretching her already taut nerves almost to breaking point.

Then she heard the sound of Neil's footsteps thudding down the stairs. 'I'll get it,' he called.

'Karen?' Moments later Neil's curt tone broke through her thoughts. 'I've just had a call from Tony.'

Fork in hand she froze and stared.

'Tony?' She heard herself repeat his name above the ringing in her ears. He couldn't have told Neil what she suspected, surely?

Neil's grave expression left her in no doubt that he had something serious to say. She swallowed hard and braced herself for the worst.

9

'Yes,' he repeated. 'Karen, my mother's been taken ill. He's phoned for the doctor.'

'Your mother?' Karen echoed, still trying to absorb the news. Then she gathered her wits together, aware of how he must be feeling. 'Oh, Neil, I am sorry. I hope she'll be all right.'

'Yes, well thanks.' His frown of concern remained in place. 'Tony insists it's nothing serious and there's no need for me to do anything but as you can understand, I've got to get over there and see her for myself.'

'Of course,' she urged. 'You must. Is there anything I can do?'

His grim smile touched her heart. How could she think he'd ever do anything dishonest? With his obvious love for those dearest to him, he would not entertain even the thought.

Whereas she, by doing such a thing, must have been crazy at the time. She prayed once the alarm of his step-mother's health was over, Tony would dismiss their earlier conversation as being ridiculous. She needed to talk to him.

'Just be here for Ellie,' Neil said. 'That's the most important thing.'

'That goes without saying,' she responded huskily.

'I know. And you won't say anything about her grandmother if she should wake.'

'Of course not. You get off and don't worry about anything else.'

Instead of turning and leaving the room, he closed the distance between them and took hold of her shoulders.

'I'm going,' he said. 'But there's just one thing. We need to do some serious talking. I've made several stupid mistakes over the past few days and there's something I've got to get off my chest.'

Their eyes locked and for a moment she thought he was going to kiss her.

Then he gave her shoulders a gentle squeeze and released her. 'I'll be back just as soon as I can.'

Alone and in something of a daze, Karen put their meal on hold and tried to fathom what it was that he had to say to her.

She smiled wryly at the hopes building up inside once again.

More than likely, as she was coming to the end of her time there he was probably going to thank her for caring for Ellie and suggest she might be able to do something similar if the need arose in the future. That was all.

Deep in thought, she wandered through to the sitting room and switched on the TV. There was bound to be something showing that would take her mind off her troubles.

A short while later she heard the sound of a vehicle pulling up outside. It couldn't be Neil, she told herself. It was far too soon.

It had to be John and Martha.

Looking forward to their company,

she pressed the remote and walked out into the hall to greet them. No doubt Martha would be bubbling over with all the details of their new grandson. She sighed. It would help to take her mind off Neil and the mystery of the coins.

Then to her surprise, the doorbell rang and kept on ringing. 'Who on earth?' she muttered to herself.

'I'm coming,' she called out loudly, although she doubted whoever it was could hear her through the solid oak door. She released the lock and pulled it open.

'Tony!' she exclaimed, pleased but confused as he stood before her carrying a black holdall. 'Neil's already gone. He left as soon as you gave him the message about his mother. You must have passed each other in the lane.'

Then the thought struck her. She frowned. What was he doing here now. It didn't make sense. 'But I don't understand. Why have you come? And how is his mother?' The questions tumbled from her lips.

'Came to see you, sweetheart,' Tony grinned, stepping over the threshold. 'Matter of fact, I did see Neil's car. I was parked off-road, making sure he was well on his way before I came to see you.'

'Parked? But why?'

'Karen? I want Dad.' The sound of Ellie's voice was an immediate distraction. Karen spun round to see she was halfway down the stairs, rubbing her eyes and looked sleepy.

'It's all right, poppet,' she called.

She quickly took the stairs before she woke completely, sure there would be some difficulty in getting her back into bed once she realised Tony was there.

Tenderly she put her arm around her shoulder and steered her the other way. 'Your dad has had to go out for a little while. He'll be back soon. Now give me your hand. It's best if you go back to bed while you're waiting.' She took Ellie's hand and guided her back up the stairs.

Karen was worried. Something wasn't right about Tony being here. She just knew it.

'In you go now and as soon as your dad gets back he'll come up to see you,' Karen promised as Ellie climbed back into bed.

Leaving the door slightly ajar in case she should wake again, she quickly made her way back downstairs. She had to get to the bottom of why Tony was here and not back at the house supporting Neil and his father.

When she saw the study door was partly open, her sense of uncertainty increased. Her stomach tensed. Tony must be checking on what she'd told him earlier, she decided.

Her hand trembled a little as she prepared herself to go inside. She did not want to confront her worst fears. Not when she knew in her heart she was in love with Neil.

Chilled to the bone, she knew she had no other choice. She needed to know. Drawing in a shaky breath, she took hold of the handle and opened the door.

As she walked into the room, her heart skipped a beat when she saw Tony behind Neil's desk bathed in the light of the angle poise lamp. The desk drawer was open.

She also noticed he'd closed the heavy brocade curtains against the evening light, which she thought was odd.

'So this is the box you believe contains the coins?' He turned it over in his hand and gave it a cursory look.

Karen's tension increased. There was something different about Tony's voice and his manner was a side of him she'd not seen before. 'Yes,' she whispered, 'that's it.'

'Let's put you of your misery, then.'

She watched with growing unease as he removed the lid. After a moment or two, he shook his head, then fixed her with a cold look. 'Well you'll probably be pleased to hear you were mistaken.'

Relief surged through her.

'As far as I'm concerned, this was a wasted journey.'

Karen's eyes widened as he took out a plain gold bangle; it's simple mellow beauty enhanced by a gold thread coiled for an inch or two around part of it.

'But I don't understand,' she gasped. She searched Tony's face for an answer.

'I do,' he said drolly. 'Simple fact is you were wrong.' He dropped the bangle back into the box and shoved it back inside the drawer. 'And as it's brand new it's of no interest to me. Had me curious though, when you rang as I'd had the coins all along. I thought my dear stepbrother must have found more and was keeping it quiet.'

As the shock of what she was hearing sank in, the strength drained out of her. She gripped the back of the chair she'd been standing behind. 'What d'you mean you had them?'

Tony gave her a self-satisfied look. 'Yes, sweetheart. I most certainly did. It's not that difficult to work out. I couldn't miss an opportunity like that now could I? Neil was asking for it just leaving them where anyone could have helped themselves.'

'But no-one else knew,' Karen defended. 'Just us.'

'You and I know that, but when I had my little chat with the police, I played on the fact that there had been a number of break-ins in the area recently. Soon had them and Neil convinced it was the same thief. Plus we'd made sure it looked like an outside job.'

We? Karen's blood ran cold.

Was Tony saying he'd been helped by someone at Mile End? But who in their right mind would do such a thing?

Then it hit her. Caroline?

No, she denied this thought immediately. She wouldn't have thrown her career and reputation away for the sake of a few gold coins. But then, she reflected, love sometimes did strange things to people and Caroline appeared to be totally smitten with Tony.

Sadness washed over her. Neil was going to be devastated when he eventually found out what had happened.

She regarded Tony with total dislike as everything began to fall into place. 'So the call about Neil's mother being taken ill wasn't true.'

'Got it in one.'

'How could you be so cruel to have him think she was?'

'He'll get over it,' Tony dismissed. 'After all he could do everything when we were kids.' His eyes narrowed. 'Even my own father thought more of him than me. Still,' he shrugged, 'I got over that a long time ago and that's enough reminiscing for tonight.'

'Problem is, what am I going to do with you? And there's little Ellie.' He paused seeming to give the matter some thought. 'But as she's tucked up in bed, the best thing would be for her to stay there.'

Relief washed over her.

Tony's eyes narrowed. 'No point in complicating the issue any more when thanks to you, things have been complicated enough.'

As he continued to regard her with contempt, her mind raced with the possibilities of how she could get out of this situation.

Her senses taut to the slightest sound or movement, they eased again when she heard a second vehicle crunch to a halt outside the study window.

It was too much to hope for that it could be Neil. But that didn't matter, she assured herself. This time it had to be John and Martha. John had said they wouldn't be late.

But, Karen frowned, how would he deal with the situation when he and Martha learned the truth. He was strong in a wiry way but he was no match for the strength of a much younger man.

'Sounds like we have company. What are you going to do now?' She brazened it out, not allowing her gaze to waver as he continued to regard her from behind the desk.

But then doubts began to niggle when she noticed he didn't seem at all bothered by this latest arrival.

When he took out a pack of cigarettes and lighter from his holdall and calmly lit one, her uncertainty increased. Her hopes of escape began to shrivel. If nothing else, it was clear Tony was in total control of his emotions.

Ears strained, it seemed like an eternity before Karen heard the front door open then was quietly closed again.

'Looks like you won't have the problem of me now, Tony,' she tried again with more courage than she knew she had. 'Once whoever's here has learned the truth, the police won't be long in coming.'

His look of amusement was unsettling. 'Karen, sweetheart,' he shook his head, 'you are such an innocent. I really wish we could have spent more time together. You'd have been a constant source of amusement.'

Anger coloured her cheeks. 'Is that right,' she snapped, breaking off to the sound of footsteps coming into the room.

She spun around. The sight of Simon standing a short distance behind her filled her with relief.

But then she remembered he was supposed to be away until Sunday night. As she took in his pale complexion and the unnaturally taut line of his strong jaw, she realised something was wrong.

Could this romance be in trouble again? But whatever had brought him back to Mile End, she was thankful for it. Tony had more than met his match with Simon's rugby-playing physique.

'Simon,' she greeted, hurrying over to him with hope in her eyes. She gripped his arm. 'You can't believe how pleased I am to see you.'

Simon shot her a look, but then instead of asking what was wrong, he frowned across the room at Tony.

'Tony,' he urged. 'What's going on?'

Tony shrugged and calmly finished his cigarette then dropped it into the small vase of wild flowers Ellie had picked for her father the day before.

Karen watched his actions with disgust.

'Nothing for you to concern yourself with, Simon,' he drawled. 'Just a minor misunderstanding on Karen's part. It's been sorted.'

Karen braced herself. Tony was not going to get away with what he'd done. 'Don't you believe him for a minute, Simon,' she protested. 'Tony has the coins. He's had them all along. I'm sorry but it looks like Caroline helped him fake the burglary.'

'Old news, Karen,' Tony came round from the other side of the desk. He leaned back against it and folded his arms. 'And you've got the facts slightly muddled. Simon's known from day one. Been such a great help. I wouldn't have been able to do it . . . and more, without him. Here, take a look at these.'

Unable to make sense of what Tony was saying, she watched as he reached for his bag again and held it open.

'Bring her over, Simon,' he instructed.

In something of a daze, she felt Simon's grip upon her arm as she was propelled forward.

'Now aren't they something?' Tony bragged.

Inside the holdall Karen could see several clear plastic bags containing dozens of gold coins that looked exactly like the ones Simon had first discovered.

'More Roman coins?' She gave both men a puzzled look.

'Aren't they just,' Tony gloated. He threw Simon a knowing look. 'After Simon found the first ones, I came back that night in the early hours to do a little digging of my own. And guess what. He'd already beaten me to it. In fact, turns out he'd been doing a little private excavation of his own for some time. Caught you red-handed, didn't I?'

Stunned, Karen turned her attention

to Simon, hoping for some kind of denial. Her heart sank when he couldn't meet her gaze.

Then she recalled the figure she'd seen out in the field on her first night at the house. She hadn't been imagining things after all. It had been Simon.

'So not wanting to upset Neil by telling him . . . ' She focused again on what Tony was saying. 'What else could I do other than go into partnership with our expert here?'

Karen found herself despising his self-satisfied expression.

'We didn't get far though, did we, Simon? That's when I thought up the idea of the burglary. After all, we were entitled to something for all our efforts and as I told him, he was the one who actually found the coins in the first place. In a sense they were really his.'

'And then bingo. Would you believe it, two nights ago we hit the jackpot and found all these hidden in some pottery. We were all set to fly to Amsterdam tonight when I got your call. I could kick myself now for wanting to come and see what you were talking about.'

Karen looked again at the coins. These more than proved Neil's feelings about the site. But it looked like they would be lost to him forever.

'I phoned Simon while you were upstairs with Ellie,' Tony broke her thoughts, 'and told him to get over here right away instead of meeting me at the airfield as we'd previously arranged. And here he is, my faithful partner in crime.'

10

'Simon,' Karen pleaded. 'Tell me it's not true.' She could barely get the words out. 'He's making this up.'

As he shook his head, Simon looked defeated. 'I can't, Karen,' he confessed. 'It's how it happened.'

Her troubled eyes searched his face. 'How could you betray Neil like this?'

Simon's remorse came out in one long sigh. Witnessing his distressed expression, Karen could only feel a huge sense of sadness. He obviously knew only too well what he'd thrown away?

'To put it simply,' he added, 'I got myself into a whole load of debt trying to impress Janine. Her parents are extremely wealthy. She's used to only the best. And d'you know what?' His short burst of laughter was bitter. 'Last week she told me it was all over. She was seeing someone else. The son of a family friend. Far more suitable in Mummy and Daddy's eyes than a struggling archaeologist.'

'The two men you saw parked in the lane are the people I owe the money to. That's why I backed up your story. Of course nobody knew the truth that they were putting the frighteners on me.'

'OK, Simon,' Tony burst in before Karen could sympathise, 'we've heard enough of your sob-story.'

'Careful what you say,' Simon responded. The flash of resentment in his eyes raised Karen's hopes. If Tony continued in the same vein Simon might turn against him.

'Don't be so touchy,' Tony dismissed. 'There are plenty more women out there. And once we've sold the coins and you're flashing your share around, they'll be coming at you from all directions. So come on,' he urged as he slackened his tie and pulled it off. 'You take the holdall. I'll use this to keep our uninvited guest's hand secure.'

'Tony,' Karen pleaded. 'Have you really thought this through. You're throwing your career away just as Simon is.'

'What career,' he snarled. 'I was suspended two weeks ago. Had a nice little money laundering business going with some American friends until some jobsworth poked their nose in. They can't prove anything but that's the end of the scam as far as I'm concerned, and no way am I going to face a disciplinary hearing. The money we get from the sale of the coins will do very nicely until I think of something else. So Karen, I'm not throwing anything away.'

And with that he pulled her around so her back was facing him.

She winced as she felt the tie dig into her skin as he quickly tied her hands together. 'Can't be too careful,' he said to Simon. 'She might try something stupid on the way out.'

The moment he spun her around again, Karen began twisting her hands in the hope of loosening the tie.

'We don't have to take Karen with us,' Simon protested vehemently, his increasing contempt of Tony clear to see. 'Can't we just leave her in the study tied to a chair or something until Neil gets back? Ellie will be on her own if we take her.'

'Oh yes, right,' Tony mocked. 'And the minute we're gone she'll probably raise the roof some way or another and wake the child.' He gave Karen a withering look. 'She's heard and seen enough. She's coming with us. Now get the bag and let's get to the airfield.'

Bundled into the back of Tony's vehicle and ordered to lie face down on the back seat, Karen resumed her efforts to release herself the moment she heard the engine roar into life. With each passing mile, as she struggled silently she became more worried about Ellie.

Once Neil realised he'd been tricked by Tony, she knew he would waste no time in driving back to Mile End. But how long would that take? Almost another hour, she reckoned.

The night was closing in and all she could hope for was that Ellie would stay asleep until morning and know nothing of what had taken place.

'Damn!' Some time later, Tony's exclamation alerted her. 'I'm sure that was the Peters who just passed us,' she heard him say to Simon.

Relief flooded through her. Once Martha and John arrived home they were bound to wonder where she and Neil were. And once they'd checked Ellie's room and discovered she was alone in the house they would know something was wrong.

Please, Neil, she pleaded silently, put two and two together and work out Tony is up to no good.

'Maybe we should turn back,' Simon suggested. 'I could bury the coins again and confess to Neil that I was behind the break-in. Give him the reason why and let him have the original ten back. You needn't come into it.'

'Oh right,' Tony jeered. 'Think it through, Simon. You're forgetting one or two little problems that will take some explaining. I made the call to get him out of the way. And Karen will tell him the truth at the first opportunity.

'No,' she heard Tony insist, 'we're sticking to the original plan and getting out of here. I need your expertise with the coins when I contact the dealers. So nothing's changed.'

'But what about Karen?' Simon insisted. 'We can't take her with us.'

'True enough. She's caused enough trouble as it is. I've some rope in the plane I'll use to tie her legs with and find something for a gag. Someone will discover her in the morning.'

When the four-by-four pulled to a sharp halt, almost jerking her off the seat, she knew they had arrived at the airfield. The surrounding silence told her it had closed for the night.

'Right, give me the bag and stay there while I get the rope,' Tony instructed Simon. 'I won't be long.'

The minute the door slammed, Karen struggled to sit up. 'Simon,' she pleaded. 'You have to do something to stop him.'

When Simon turned in his seat and looked at her, she was shocked by how drawn he looked.

'Give me the chance to escape and I'll run to the inn. It's not that far. I could contact the police while you try to overcome Tony.'

Her heart sank when Simon grimaced. 'I can't take the risk. He could recapture you and there's no telling what he might do then. Beneath all that charm, he's got a temper I wouldn't like you to be on the wrong side of. Believe me, Karen, it's going to be all right.'

'But how can it be?' she flung back at him. 'Once you get inside his plane there'll be no turning back. Your reputation will be ruined.'

Simon's wry look was disheartening. 'I'd say it already is. I won't be staying in Holland. Once we've landed, I'll give him the slip and make my way back. I owe that much to Neil.'

'But Tony will have the coins,' she exclaimed.

'Karen, believe me. I can't explain right now but it's going to be OK.'

She refused to accept his reasoning. Determination overcame pain as she made one final effort to loosen the tie. Satisfaction boosted her hopes when she finally managed to pull one hand free.

Bracing herself, she reached for the door and flung it open. As her feet touched the ground, Simon's cry of surprised urged her on. Thankful for her dark clothes, she fled off the runway on to the grassed area where the light aircraft were parked, her mind racing as quickly as her feet.

Desperately she hoped the planes would give some cover before she reached the boundary hedge. And if she kept to that she might not be seen so easily.

But the dark starless night foiled her intentions and all too soon she lost her sense of direction.

Turning again, she ran through a gap between the planes when the shock of being brought down by a rugby tackle knocked the breath from her body.

'Stay there and don't move,' she heard Simon's frantic instruction before an even darker blackness overcame her.

★　★　★

When the sound of several voices stirred her senses. Karen tried desperately to open her eyes. Confusion filled her mind. Beneath half-closed lids, she eventually realised she was lying down, covered by a blanket and there were people busily occupied beside her.

She tried to turn to see what was happening then gasped when a bolt of pain shot through her head.

'Karen?'

Her heart turned over. Now she was hearing things, she told herself groggily. Neil couldn't be here. Wherever here was. He was with his mother. And with that thought the events of the evening came flooding back. Simon? Tony? She began to panic. Where were they?

She moved again. She needed to know.

'Karen? Lie still. Everything's all right. You're safe now.'

The soft caring tone she'd just imagined was there again. She struggled to open her eyes fully and this time succeeded.

Neil was sitting at her side. And as her eyes focused on his rugged looks, the raw concern darkening his gaze sent a warm glow coursing through her.

'Thank heaven,' he said. 'You're back with me again.'

'Where . . . ' She tried again but couldn't manage the rest.

'We're in an ambulance. The paramedics are almost finished with Simon then you'll be taken to the hospital. Don't worry. It won't be long now.'

'Simon's here? Not in the plane?' she croaked.

'Yes,' Neil assured her. 'He's lying just across from you.'

'Is he all right?'

Neil nodded. 'Apart from a nasty bang on the head and I should imagine a whole lot of bruises, he's doing fine.'

'Neil?' Needing the physical reassurance of his strength, she pulled out her hand from beneath the blanket. Without her having to say another word, his strong fingers curved over her own.

Then as the whole mental picture of what she'd been through filled her mind, she struggled to sit up.

'Ellie,' she gasped. 'Who's looking after her.'

'Careful, Karen.' Neil quickly supported her shoulders. 'You mustn't try to sit up yet.' Carefully he lowered her back against the pillow. 'Martha and John are with her.'

Karen frowned. 'Ellie was up when they got back?'

Neil's mouth hardened. 'She was. That's one thing I'll never forgive Tony for. But more about that later.'

'OK, Professor, we'll be on our way now,' one of the paramedics said before

Karen had a chance to say another word.

'You just sit tight there while we get these two off to hospital.' He turned to Karen and gave her an encouraging smile. 'No broken bones. But you'll both need a more thorough check just to be on the safe side.'

Carefully, Karen turned her head towards where Simon lay. Concern marked her brow when she saw his eyes were closed, his face deathly pale and he had a huge wad of dressings on his head.

'I'm worried about Simon,' she whispered to Neil, 'he looks so pale.'

Neil grimaced. 'Tony knocked him out. From what we can gather, there was a fight. Tony took off just as the police and I got here. Escaped by the skin of his teeth.'

'Oh no,' Karen groaned, 'the coins.'

'Don't you worry about another thing,' Neil chided gently. 'All you have to think about is getting plenty of rest. I'll explain everything later.'

'Ellie's been fast asleep for hours so there's no need for you to worry about checking on her,' Martha said, after greeting all three on their return from the hospital.

Neil had insisted she held on to his arm after getting out of the car. He drew closer to her. 'It's the sitting room first,' he insisted. 'I think we all need to take some time out to catch our breath.'

Martha opened the sitting room door for them then with Neil's tender guidance, Karen was led to one of the sofas.

'Thanks, Martha.' Neil still held Karen's hand until she was settled. 'Now tea all around, I should think. How about you, Simon?'

'Anything at all,' he responded quietly.

Simon, Karen worried, still appeared in something of a daze, even though Neil had told her his X-rays had shown no damage to his skull.

'Tea it is then,' Neil said briskly. 'Now Simon, get yourself into one of those chairs and relax,' he instructed after Martha had left the room.

The grateful look Simon shot him, sent a wave of sympathy over Karen. His drawn expression revealed how tense he was feeling.

'I'll be back in a minute,' Neil said. He gave her the smile she was coming to adore. I know you won't be happy until I've checked Ellie again.'

'I've well and truly blown it, haven't I?' Simon sighed when they were alone. 'I can't believe Neil is still prepared to have me here now he knows what I've done.'

'I'm sure Neil is very fair minded,' Karen insisted.

'You've no objections to Karen sitting in on this, have you?' Neil asked Simon when he returned. 'And yes,' he threw her a smile, 'she's fine,' he added, answering her unspoken question.

'Of course, I haven't,' Simon responded. He gave her a wry smile. 'Sorry you were involved in what happened tonight. After what you've been through you're entitled to hear the rest.'

'My thoughts entirely,' Neil agreed.

After Martha returned with a tray of tea things and served everybody before saying goodnight, Neil settled back on the sofa alongside Karen. When he linked his fingers with hers she felt it was the most natural thing in the world.

'OK, Simon,' he encouraged, 'perhaps you'd like to pick up from just before I arrived with the police.'

'Right. For what it's worth . . . '

Karen sensed he was ready now to get it all off his chest but she was still concerned on his behalf. For all her attempts at reassuring him, she still wondered, as the police were involved, what was going to happen to him after tonight?

He put his cup and saucer down on the low table. 'Sorry about bringing you down like that, Karen. Tony was so furious when he realised you'd escaped, I was worried about your safety if he found you first.'

Karen shivered and tried not to think about the darker side of Tony which she'd already been a victim of. She pulled her thoughts back to what Simon was saying.

'I told him you'd run off in the opposite direction to the one I knew you'd taken. He wasn't to know. He started calling me all the fools under the sun and the next moment he was laying into me with what felt like a spanner.'

Karen couldn't believe what she was hearing. She glanced at Neil to see his face was like thunder.

'I gave him as good as I got,' Simon defended, 'but then the next thing I knew I was coming to in the ambulance.' He shrugged. 'It must have been his intention to use it on me anyway and fly off alone. Despite what he'd said about needing my expertise when we came to sell the coins.'

'I'll take up the rest, Simon.' Neil said as Simon began to look fatigued from the efforts of talking. 'You take it easy for a moment.'

He turned to Karen. 'John rang me on my mobile as soon as he and Martha got back and found Ellie alone.' She noticed his jaw tightened and felt the pressure of his hand increase. 'She was sitting on the landing extremely upset. Told Martha and John she'd heard someone shouting.'

'Sorry. That would have been me and Tony,' Simon said with some regret.

'I'd left her bedroom door open a little,' Karen explained. 'She was unsettled and I thought the light from the landing would reassure her.'

Neil nodded. 'It seems that when she walked out on to the landing she recognised Tony's voice but was confused and troubled because he was shouting. So she stayed up there not knowing what to do.'

'But she's all right now?' Karen needed to hear this again.

'She's fine,' he smiled. 'Sleeping like a baby.'

'But Tony's got away with it, hasn't he?' she insisted. 'All those coins. They must be worth a fortune.'

'Simon?' Neil prompted. 'I think it's about time we put Karen out of her misery.'

'He doesn't have the coins, Karen,' Simon said. 'He has several bags of sugar.'

'Sugar?' She looked at him wide-eyed.

'I'd helped Tony pack the coins so I knew exactly the type of bag he was using. I bought another, weighted it with sugar before I left to meet up with him and prayed I'd have the opportunity to switch them and somehow get away.'

He grimaced. 'The call he made telling me there'd been a slight change of plan was disconcerting. He wouldn't go into detail. Just told me to get over here right away. Then when I saw you I wondered how it would all end. I couldn't believe my luck when he insisted I carry out the bag when we left while he saw to you. While he was bundling you into the vehicle, I made the swap.'

'How on earth did you do that?' Karen frowned. 'You weren't carrying a bag when you arrived.'

He smiled and for the first time that night, a hint of the Simon she knew returned. 'I'd left it at the side of the porch, hidden from view. Tony was preoccupied with you when we came out. I realised it had to be then. I took my chances when he was bundling you into his vehicle and switched them over.'

'So the coins were here all the time?' Karen looked at Neil and Simon in turn.

'Never left Mile End,' Neil confirmed. 'Simon told me about the two bags while you were still unconscious. Because of the obvious injury to his head, I thought he was rambling, but I rang John and told him to go outside and see if there was a bag there. And,' he smiled, 'sure enough, there was. I instructed him to open it and the rest you know.'

'I wonder where Tony is now?' Karen said.

Neil's expression grew grim again. 'Knowing my stepbrother, I expect he'd take the first opportunity to gloat over his expected fortune the moment he landed.'

'Then by now he'll be in a state of shock, I should imagine,' Simon concluded with some satisfaction.

'No more than he deserves,' Neil gritted. 'He got more than he bargained for by trying to double-cross you, Simon.'

'Well, it's gone some way into making up for betraying you,' he muttered, looking away.

'Acting more like a complete idiot I'd say is more apt,' Neil contradicted. 'Why on earth didn't you come to me in the first place? I'd have done my best to help you out.' Neil sighed. 'We'll talk some more tomorrow. Right now you look all in. Best thing for you is to get yourself off to bed.'

Simon's expression brightened. 'You mean you're still prepared to have me here after all that's happened.'

Neil gave him a wry look. 'Looks like it, doesn't it? Now go on, before I change my mind,' he added gruffly.

As Simon closed the door behind him, Karen's worries were still there to see. 'Neil, what's going to happen to him?'

He gave her a half-smile. 'Not a great deal. I'll convince the police he was just as much a victim as you were. We have the coins so in one sense, nothing has actually been stolen. He's been a total idiot of course, but then,' he paused and captured her eyes, 'love can make the most stable person do or even believe the craziest of things.

'We'll have a real head to head tomorrow and iron things out. I wouldn't want to lose him from the team. He's an excellent archaeologist with a great future ahead of him.'

Once more Karen felt the pressure of

his fingers tighten against her own.

'Everyone's allowed one mistake, surely,' he murmured. 'Like I so foolishly did over you seeing those men in the lane. Will you ever forgive me for doubting you?'

'Of course,' she began huskily, her cheeks warming as she remembered the gold bangle.

Hadn't she done exactly the same as Neil?

She had to tell him. She swallowed. 'But I have my own confession to make. And it far outstrips your lack of faith in me.'

His brow furrowed markedly. 'Karen? What are you going to say?'

'I saw you the day you went into Chester. Ellie and I were photographing the Eastgate Clock. You were gone again before I could draw your attention. When we came down off the walls and passed the gallery I'd seen you going inside, I must admit I was curious. And then when we got back and came into your study . . .' She broke off.

This was so difficult to put into words. 'I saw a flash of gold before you closed the box.'

'Oh, that,' he said, suddenly looking a little sheepish.

'It's so ridiculous now, but I thought they were the original coins Simon found and you'd had them all along.' There, she'd said it.

'You thought that?' he said quietly.

Unable to meet his gaze, she braced herself for his outrage. But it didn't come. Instead he got up from the sofa. 'Don't move,' he instructed firmly. 'I'll be back in a minute.'

Puzzled, she did as she was told until he reappeared carrying the very box she'd mentioned. He dropped down beside her again and removed the lid. Inside, the bangle gleamed richly against the purple velvet lining.

Karen caught her breath. 'It's absolutely beautiful.'

'I'm glad you think so. It's a copy of a Graeco-Roman bangle, about 200 AD. Although it's not as beautiful as the person I bought it for.'

He held it up. 'I hope it fits.'

'For me,' she gasped, staring back at him in disbelief as he took hold of her hand again and carefully slid the bangle up on to her wrist.

'Of course it's for you,' he murmured. 'Who else d'you think I'd bought it for?' His tone grew serious as he captured her eyes again. 'I fooled myself into believing I was buying you a thank-you gift for the wonderful care you've given Ellie. Then I faced up to the truth. There's no thank-you about this at all. It's a total declaration of how I feel about you.'

'Oh, Neil.' As his words sank in Karen felt the sting of tears and his handsome features blurred before her.

'I practically fell in love with you the very first moment I saw you,' he went on. 'Like an idiot I fought those feelings. I never believed it could happen so quickly.'

Karen sighed and touched the bangle lovingly. 'And I still feel awful about thinking what I did.'

'Good,' he teased, 'that makes us about equal.' He slipped his arm around her shoulders and drew her closer to him. As he placed a kiss on her temple, she wriggled closer and slipped her arm around him. 'Seriously, though,' he said, 'if you hadn't phoned Tony, chances are Simon might not have had the opportunity to switch the bags before Tony attacked him.'

'So it's all worked out well in the end,' she sighed happily.

'Not quite.' Neil reached up with his other hand and tilted her chin. Devilment lit his eyes. 'Just the small matter of hearing you say you love me too, and if so, setting the date.'

'Of course I love you,' she confessed.

'It feels like I've been waiting for this moment for ever,' he murmured.

We do hope that you have enjoyed reading this large print book.

Did you know that all of our titles are available for purchase?

We publish a wide range of high quality large print books including:
Romances, Mysteries, Classics
General Fiction
Non Fiction and Westerns

Special interest titles available in large print are:
The Little Oxford Dictionary
Music Book, Song Book
Hymn Book, Service Book

Also available from us courtesy of Oxford University Press:
Young Readers' Dictionary
(large print edition)
Young Readers' Thesaurus
(large print edition)

For further information or a free brochure, please contact us at:
Ulverscroft Large Print Books Ltd.,
The Green, Bradgate Road, Anstey,
Leicester, LE7 7FU, England.
Tel: (00 44) **0116 236 4325**
Fax: (00 44) **0116 234 0205**

FALSE PRETENCES

Phyllis Humphrey

When Ginger Maddox, a San Francisco stock-broker, meets handsome Neil Cameron, she becomes attracted to him. But then mysterious things begin to happen, involving Neil's aunts. After a romantic weekend with Neil, Ginger overhears a telephone conversation confirming her growing suspicions that he's involved in illegal trading. She's devastated, fearing that this could end their relationship. But it's the elderly aunts who help show the young people that love will find a way.